DEATH FROM
TWO DIRECTIONS

Too late Robert Sand saw the rattlesnake. Its flat, hideous head snapped forward like a whip, its fangs digging into Sand's left forearm, the needles of pain tearing into his flesh and moving swiftly into his body.

Even as the Black Samurai's sword decapitated the rattler with a swift backhand stroke, he felt the deadly venom begin to work within him. At that same moment, he saw the huge figure of Mangas Salt, the killer warrior, appear in the doorway, his battle ax gleaming in his hand.

"Too late, samurai," said Mangas Salt. As the giant moved forward for the kill, the air was shattered by his triumphant battle yell, "*Aieeeee!*"

Had Robert Sand, Black Samurai, finally met his master . . . ?

Other SIGNET Books You'll Want to Read

KILLER WARRIOR

Third in the
BLACK SAMURAI series

by
Marc Olden

A SIGNET BOOK

NEW AMERICAN LIBRARY

TIMES MIRROR

SIGNET, SIGNET CLASSICS, MENTOR, PLUME AND MERIDIAN BOOKS
are published by The New American Library, Inc.,
1301 Avenue of the Americas, New York, New York 10019

FIRST PRINTING, JULY, 1974

1 2 3 4 5 6 7 8 9

PRINTED IN THE UNITED STATES OF AMERICA

CONTENTS

CHAPTER 1

An Old Arabian Custom

Zaki, 22, small, slender, with uncombed thick black hair, quickly brought the rifle up to his unshaven brown cheek and sighted at a dim yellow light bulb tied to a twisted dirty green cord hanging from the ceiling. He pulled the trigger. Click!

Laughing, the young Arab terrorist lowered the empty rifle, holding it across his stomach and smiling down at it, his bright brown eyes racing from its black barrel lightly coated with oil back to the dark-brown wooden stock.

His small head snapped back with laughter. "Jew killer. This I call Jew killer."

Gamal smiled. "Call it the American Jew killer," he said. "These are American guns. I mean, they *used* to be American guns." His lean, delicate hands patted the dark-green wooden crate he had ripped open with a crowbar minutes ago. He had a long face, made longer by greased sideburns reaching down to his jawbone. Even when he smiled, he looked sad.

"Guns and money," said short, 24-year-old Ben-Salam. "Tonight we have both." Everything he wore, from dirty white sweater to black-and-white sneakers, was pushed out of shape by his fat, lumpy body.

The three Arab terrorists were in a small garage in one of Paris' rundown ghettos inhabited entirely by poor Algerians and Africans. At ten o'clock that night, the Arabs had met two Frenchmen who had been selling them guns for almost a year. Tonight had been just another scheduling of illegal guns and instant cash.

That had been 45 minutes ago.

Tonight, the Arabs had severed the business arrangement.

They had done this by shooting the two Frenchmen in the back of the head four times and taking the two cases of M-16 rifles they had originally agreed to buy for $15,000.

Now the three young Arabs were alone with the two opened cases of rifles, talking and laughing easily among themselves.

"We have new rifles but we need new Frenchmen," said Zaki, and he joined the other two in laughing at his own remark.

Yawning, fat Ben-Salam said, "I'm hungry. Let's hide the guns, then eat."

Nodding agreement, the other two turned toward the rifles, their brown hands stroking the guns once more, their eyes bright with their new killing power.

Their backs were turned and none of the three young Arabs saw a huge black shadow move from the darkness and slide silently across the floor toward them. It was Gamal, the lean, long-faced terrorist, who sensed something, and still bending over the rifles, he stiffened.

His fingers inched toward the Erma Werke Luger .22 jammed in his belt. Gripping the butt hard, he spun around to face the shadow, the heads of the two other Arabs snapping quickly toward him, then toward the shadow.

The razor-sharp steel blade of a small ax gleamed brightly under the dim yellow bulb, moving toward Gamal's throat with frightening speed and power. As his gun came free of his faded brown pants, the steel blade tore into his throat, cutting away all sound, and life.

Blood jetted upward, turning the left side of the Arab's lean face bright red, as his body fell backward onto a case of rifles. The handgun clattered to the dirty black oil-stained concrete floor.

In that instant before death reached for them as well, Zaki and Ben-Salam froze with shock and horror at the incredible figure moving at them swiftly.

They had only seconds to stare, cry aloud, then move in desperation and panic.

A bare-chested Apache Indian, huge, muscular, horrifying, stood in front of them, bloody ax in his hand. A thick black headband across his forehead held long coarse black hair in place. A two-inch-wide streak of white paint ran across the bridge of his nose and under both eyes.

His mouth was a long, thin slash in the dark-brown skin of his flat-featured, cruel face. Buckskin leggings were wrapped tightly around the Indian's powerful thighs and calves, and on his enormous feet were dark-brown moccasins.

Zaki's face, pop-eyed with fear, turned quickly toward the small, dust-covered truck, where his American Colt .45 lay on the front seat. In a flurry of arms and legs, his small body charged with fear, he ran for the front of the truck.

With almost nothing more than a flick of his thick wrist, the huge Indian sent the small ax flying, turning it over once in midair. His throw was accurate and powerful. The blade bit deep into the small Arab's back, driving him forward faster. His body hit the side of the truck, then bounced off and fell face down.

The Indian turned to the last Arab.

Ben-Salam's gun was in his hand, but as his finger tightened on the trigger, pain raced along his arm and up to his shoulder.

A powerful kick from the huge Indian's right leg had broken his elbow. The gun went flying several feet away in darkness, and Ben-Salam shook his head side to side in silent pleading as the Indian stepped closer.

The Indian's left hand shot out, pressing down hard on top of the fat Arab's skull. His right hand roughly cupped the Arab's jaw, and then in one brutal move, the Indian quickly turned the Arab's head as though turning the wheel of a car.

There was a dry snapping sound as Ben-Salam's neck broke, and the last noise he made was a long sigh as though he was thankful the last 30 seconds of hell had ended. He was on his knees, his head still in the Indian's hands.

Once more, the powerful man turned the head farther until it reached an ugly angle impossible in the living. Satisfied the Arab was dead, the Indian dropped his body to the floor.

Behind him, he heard a moan. Zaki. He was crawling nowhere in particular, the small ax sticking out from his back like the fin of a dolphin. In less than two seconds, the Indian was standing over him.

Yanking the bloody ax from Gamal's back, the Indian raised it high, then drove it deep into the base of the dying man's skull.

The three Arab terrorists were dead, but the lesson of their death must not be lost. There was more to do.

Again, the huge, silent Indian lifted the bloody ax high over his head, muscles bunching tightly in his powerful brown shoulders, arms, and back, as he brought the blade down in a devastating blow.

Thwack!

Beads of sweat shone on his forehead like bits of glass. Grunting with satisfaction, he raised the bright red ax again, bringing it down as hard as he could.

Abdus Faisal sipped the chilled white wine slowly, enjoying the coolness filling his mouth, letting it slide easily down his throat, feeling the coolness turn slowly to warmth in his stomach. He was naked, lying on black silk sheets in a Paris apartment paid for by his embassy, where he worked as a clerk.

His plump left hand, two diamond rings glittering in the room light, stroked the perfumed, naked flesh of the fifteen-year-old boy prostitute lying in bed beside him. Faisal had paid for the boy himself. Why not? Paris was expensive, but Faisal lived well, enjoying the best of foods, wines, and beautiful young boys. A phone call to a retired top French general nicknamed "The Recruiter," now supplementing his retirement income by procuring the most beautiful young male flesh in Paris, was all that was needed to send a skilled, willing lover to the Arab's doorstep.

This one was named Richard, and Faisal had had him before. After sex, the young boy would always fall asleep, his delicate pretty head on Faisal's chest, his thin arms wrapped around the plump Arab's neck. Faisal liked that; it always made him feel as though no money were involved, that Richard had made love because he cared.

Later, the boy would awake, dress, and leave without a word.

And always, Faisal would wait until the last minute before giving the beautiful boy 2,500 francs. Anything to make it appear as though the boy had actually been a lover, not a prostitute.

The telephone jarred the Arab from his world of sense pleasures. Frowning in annoyance, he looked down at the sleeping, naked boy in his arms, then gently shifted to a half-sitting position. The phone rang again. Placing the almost empty wine glass down on a black granite table top, he reached out for the silver-coated antique phone.

As he picked up the receiver, Richard stirred, moved away from Faisal, and turning his back to the Arab, continued to sleep.

Whispering harshly, the Arab said in French, "Damn it, who the hell is this? Do you know what time it is?"

A firm but gentle voice answered in French, "Eleven-eighteen at night, precisely."

In a motion quick with fear and nervousness, Faisal sat straight up in bed, his elbow knocking the wine glass off the table and onto the thick green carpet. That voice. In seconds, the Arab felt cold, and his mouth went dry as though he were back home walking barefoot across the hot desert.

The voice belonged to Valbonne, a terrifying man who sold guns to anyone with money. Valbonne. Incredibly wealthy, never seen by anyone except a handful of associates, a man more deadly than the weapons he sold. Valbonne. A mysterious Frenchman living in Switzerland, who did business the world over.

Valbonne, who killed and tortured to keep his business of guns flowing smoothly as blood oozing from an open wound.

Faisal licked his suddenly dry lips. Gripping the receiver tightly with two perspiring hands, he said, "M-Mr. Valbonne. Forgive me, I did not know it was you. I—"

Valbonne's quiet voice, empty of any emotion, slithered into the Arab's ear like a hissing snake ready to strike. "Conversations bore me, Faisal. This one will be as brief as possible. Tonight, two of my men met to conclude a business transaction with three of your countrymen who colorfully describe themselves as freedom fighters. The transaction was to involve $15,000 in American money and two cases of my merchandise."

Faisal nodded his head in agreement, still listening quietly. He had put the Arab terrorist organization in touch with Valbonne, just as he had helped other gun-hungry Arabs reach the mysterious Frenchman. To kill Jews, you needed guns, needed them quickly without questions being asked. Had something gone wrong? Had there been a doublecross?

Valbonne always had guns, any kind, in any amount. But his prices were high and he dealt strictly in cash. Attempts to cheat him out of either guns or money inevitably brought down a legendary brutality, turning the cheat into pitiful victim. The Frenchman was a hard man in a hard world.

His cruelty, power and influence equaled that of heads of government. Hell, Valbonne was a government!

"Mr. Valbonne, if something went wrong tonight, believe me it wasn't my fault. I would never—"

"Yes, Faisal," said the soft voice. *"You* would never. But your three countrymen *did,* or tried to. Unfortunately for me, I must sometimes do business with those who come recommended by others. I took your word about this organization of so-called freedom fighters. Their business was not excessive. I no more need them than you need a woman to make you happy."

Faisal's heart jumped and he looked across the bed at the slim naked boy sleeping on the black silken sheets. Valbonne had eyes everywhere. The Arab had heard that again and again, but this was the first time that fact had been shoved down his throat.

"Mr. Valbonne—"

"Please, Faisal. I'll soon finish and you can go back to your specific tastes. Your countrymen disposed of my men and removed the merchandise. Meaning I was cheated twice; out of my merchandise and out of money. An associate managed to retrieve both. I believe there is a custom in Arabian countries whereby thieves are severely reminded that one should never steal."

Custom? Faisal licked his lips, his fleshy brown face wrinkled tight with swift unanswered questions. What the hell was the Frenchman talking about? The Arab's right hand nervously rubbed his own fat naked thigh.

"Faisal, please put the phone down and go to the small balcony. Now."

Faisal nodded his head in agreement, his mind racing, his heart pounding. He had never met the Frenchman, had only spoken to him over the phone during the past three years, but he was as terrified of him as if he had been standing at the foot of the bed with a machine gun pointed at the Arab's groin.

Laying the receiver down on the black granite table top, the fat Arab rolled awkwardly out of bed and moved across the thick green carpet, his naked brown body smooth with fat.

His apartment was on the top floor of a small five-story building on Boulevard St. Germain, and sitting on the small balcony on a warm day was another of the pleasures he allowed himself. Pulling open the two glass-and-wooden doors, he stepped outside into the April chill, his body trembling with cold and apprehension.

His feet brushed something in the darkness. In the street below him, he heard the honking of taxi horns and a woman's high-pitched laughter. Stiffly, the fat Arab bent over and touched the thing at his feet.

A brown burlap bag, almost black-colored in the night, damp in spots and wired tightly closed. Holding it high, Faisal frowned at it, then came back into the room, leaving the balcony doors open. Carrying the burlap bag over to the bed, he picked up the telephone receiver and said, "Mr. Valbonne, it's—"

"I know what it is, Faisal. I want *you* to know what it is. Open it."

The fat Arab laid the receiver back down on the table top, then with fat, nervous fingers began to unwind the thin black wire keeping the brown, dark-stained burlap bag closed. Twice the wire pierced his finger, and each time he brought the finger to his mouth, sucking the blood.

Something was wrong. He felt it. Something was *wrong*.

The wire came free, dropping to the green carpet. Behind him, he heard Richard's even breathing, the boy sleeping as though at home in his own room. Faisal's hand caressed the bag, brushing over the firm objects inside. What was in it? Obviously Valbonne wanted him to know, but why go to all this trouble?

His back to Richard, Faisal leaned over and placed the burlap bag on the rug, emptying the contents on the thick green carpet.

The Arab's eyes went wide with horror, and the sour, acrid taste of the food he had eaten less than two hours ago swept into his throat. Both of his hands covered his mouth, but not in time to stop the vomit pouring from his mouth and nose.

He sank to his knees, the warm slush of half-digested food sliding down his face, arms and chest. His heart jumped and tried to batter its way free from his chest. The fat Arab knelt on the green rug, and his body jerked again and again with sudden sickness and paralyzing fear.

On the rug in front of him were three severed hands, the front and back of each streaked red with blood.

Tears slid down his fat face into the warm sour-smelling food that seconds ago had been inside him.

Dazed, he turned to the phone, stared at it, then slowly reached out, picked it up, and placed it to his ear. As he tightly gripped the receiver, the vomit squeezed out between his fat fingers. His breathing was hoarse and loud, as though he had run ten miles.

"In your country, the custom is to cut off the hands of thieves," said Valbonne. "They lived as Arabs, and I assure you they died the same way. For the time being, I am satisfied you were no part of their exercise in futility. Should I feel differently, you shall share their traditions. All of them. One final thing, Faisal. If I take your recommendation on anyone, anyone at all, I hold you personally responsible for that person. Do you understand?"

Nodding his head, the fat Arab whispered, "Yes, Mr. Valbonne."

"Anyone who deals with me is responsible for a certain integrity, shall we say," said the Frenchman. "Please remember this." Click. The phone went dead.

Still on his knees, the fat Arab gripped the phone, his tear-filled eyes staring straight ahead, unwilling to look down at the bloody horror near his knees.

Had he looked through the open balcony doors, he would have perhaps seen the faint outline of a tall, powerful bare-chested figure standing in darkness on a roof directly across from his apartment. His dark-brown eyes peering through the darkness separating the two buildings, the figure stood silently watching the Arab.

In the cool Paris April night, only the tall man's fingers moved, gently brushing the cold steel blade on the small ax tucked in the front of his belt.

CHAPTER 2

Training

The young black man and the old Japanese man were alone in the small, unheated dojo, their feet scraping across the worn yellow straw mats. Robert Sand, the black man, moved in swift powerful karate techniques. The small white-haired Japanese man, his face aged and wrinkled like a lemon too long in the sun, circled around him, observing, correcting, criticizing.

Sand had prepared carefully for this month, 30 days of special karate and judo training in the small town of Okai, Japan. His sensei, his teacher, for these 30 days was Master Kisao, 79 years old and a former comrade of Master Konuma, the man who had accepted Sand for Samurai training almost eight years ago. Konuma was dead now, brutally murdered, his murder avenged by Sand.

Several letters and inquiries were necessary to locate Master Kisao, followed by more letters to arrange a personal meeting. Years ago Kisao had trained with Master Konuma, and like him, had retired to a small village to live out his days in peace. He did not train much any more, nor did he accept students.

Kisao did train a little. In letters exchanged with his old comrade Konuma, he had learned of the extraordinary black man Konuma was training as a Samurai. He had remembered Konuma's praise of Robert Sand. That's why he had agreed to see the black Samurai, to give him special training. Above all, Kisao wanted to talk with someone who had known his old comrade.

The training was brutal. Intense and concentrated, seven days a week, with emphasis equally on technique and concentration. Both men spoke only Japanese, and for a week Sand had found it difficult again to eat a diet of all Japanese food. After a week, raw fish, rice, and seaweed tasted good, and the hard training lifted his heart back to his happy, satisfying years with Master Konuma and the Japanese men Sand had learned to call brothers.

No doubt about it, Western living was too easy. "In the West, you do not walk, you ride," said Master Kisao. "That is bad. Must walk. A man must walk. Strengthens his legs. Why do you sit on chairs in the West? You must remember, because you are much Japanese, no? Sit on the floor. Remember."

The black man smiled. It wasn't easy to sit on the floor all the time, but the old man was right. Life was too easy in the West. Too easy. What wasn't easy were the occasional feelings Sand had of not knowing who he was. He was black and American, yet he had spent the most important part of his life in the Far East, training intensely to become a fighting warrior belonging to another century.

He smiled again. Black Samurai. Well, it wasn't always confusing. He felt much better when he just accepted the fact that his life was different and would always be so. As long as he had the strength he could do and be what he wanted. Accept it, that was the best way. And don't sit on chairs.

Today, he had gotten out of bed at four in the morning, run five miles through the small darkened village, out into the fields and along the dirt road leading to the highway. He enjoyed the quiet, the peace and the feeling that once more, he was pushing his heart and body to the limit.

Memories of his Samurai brothers and Master Konuma flashed across his mind as he ran through the cold darkness, and for a few seconds, his heart ached with the pain of knowing he would never see them again. Putting that out of his mind, he ran, sweat trickling down his face and neck.

Today's practice was unusual. "Left side," said Kisao, his wrinkled old face smiling at the thought of the difficulties Sand would soon have. "You right-handed, so today we practice left side. Punch, kick, defend, attack all with left side. You must be even strong." The old man grinned.

They began. Sand punched the air with his left hand, slow at first so the old man could see. "Tighten fist. Don't keep your fingers loose."

Tightening his fist, the black man continued to punch, a little faster, then at a sharp command from the old man, he punched with all of his speed and power, his sweat-dampened karate uniform snapping with the precision of his punch.

"Right fist," said the old man. "Draw it back more, all the way, and keep your elbow down more. Down." More punches, over and over, again and again, the old man's small slanted eyes missing nothing. Sand's arm ached at the shoulder and his elbow burned with fatigue. "Faster," said the old man. "You are slowing down. Faster." Tensing his face, his lips pressed tightly together with determination, the black Samurai threw a murderous punch at an imaginary opponent in front of him.

That night, he fell exhausted into bed, careful to lie on his back or on his right side. His left arm and leg felt as though someone had been scraping at the muscle and nerves with broken glass.

The next morning. More running, his left leg moving stiffly but not hurting as much as it had last night. A light breakfast of fruit and rice, followed by 45 minutes of cleaning the small practice area by himself. Seconds after he finished, the old man stood in the doorway.

In both hands, he held chains. "Come. This morning you practice outside."

Ten minutes later, the black Samurai stood in front of a thick tree on top of a small hill overlooking the river. Behind him, the sound of the water rushing over rocks was as sharp and as clear as the chilled early-morning air he breathed.

The chains were attached to a steel hook imbedded in the bark of the thick tree, and he stood holding the ends, a few inches of chain wrapped around each wrist.

In a soft voice, the old man commanded, "Now."

And swiftly, as though trying to flip a man or perhaps pull the tree out of the ground by its roots, the black man turned his back to the tree, bending his knees forward until they almost touched the ground, leaning as far forward as he could go. He pulled on the chains with all his strength.

Cold steel links cut into his hands. The muscles of his bare back bunched up and the veins leaped from his neck.

"Stop," said the old man.

Sand relaxed, letting the chains slack.

"That is how you must do your throwing techniques. You must turn fast, even faster than you did. Above all, you must have total commitment to the throw. Hands, legs, the whole body must be in the throw. And your mind, you must use all of your mind, just as you did just now. Now again, this time faster."

The cold wind blew across Sand's bare chest, now damp with perspiration. Gripping the chains tightly, he took a deep breath, then with an incredible burst of speed, pivoted, yelling "Kiaaaii!" and pulling on both chains as hard as he could.

Ping!

One chain burst, several links flying through the darkness.

The black Samurai fell forward to one knee, one end of the broken chain in his hand, the other end of the chain on the ground behind him. Breathing hard, he looked at the old man, now standing with his mouth slightly opened in surprise. Quickly, the old man recovered, looking from the tree, then to the black man now on one knee staring at him, muscular black chest heaving with his mighty effort.

Bowing his head slightly, the old man said softly, "Samurai!"

Sand's hands were bleeding, and there was a sharp pain across his back. But with a mixture of humility and pride, he lowered his head and answered, "Thank you, sensei."

He had five more days to go when the message arrived. He slept in Master Kisao's small, plain home, and that's where the message found him. Late at night, a car pulled up and a fat Japanese man with blue-tinted eyeglasses walked up the red-and-gray flagstone walk and knocked on the door.

He waited while Sand read the cable. "Emergency. Important. Imperial Hotel. Mr. Gray."

Mr. Gray. Code name for William Baron Clarke, for-

mer President of the United States, a Texan with
$500 million, plus a strong sense of justice, and an in-
credibly up-to-date file on people he called "sumbitches
with power and a whole lot of mean in their bones."

William Baron Clarke. Nicknamed the Baron. More
than a Texan with a fat wallet, he was also a man who
had molded the acquisition and use of power into an art.
He knew power, loved it, caressed it with hands and
heart, but at the age of 64 realized that unless he did some
good with it, there would be no point to his life.

Together, he and Robert Sand had gone after those
who used power to destroy others while enriching themselves. "You got the skill, the balls and the brains, son,"
he'd said to Sand. "I got the money and the power and I
got my fingers and eyeballs everywhere. Together we can
pull somebody's foot off somebody else's throat."

They had teamed to destroy the men who had killed
the black Samurai's 22 Samurai brothers and Master Konuma.

But there were others who needed destroying.

And that's what the message was about.

And with the Baron, emergency meant exactly that.

The taxi driver watched with eyes hidden behind blue-
tinted glasses. He had been told to wait.

In his room, Sand packed his few things swiftly, looked
around the room once more, feeling the pain of leaving
something close to him. In a sense, it was like leaving
Konuma over again. As he turned to walk through the
door, Kisao stood silently in front of him.

Sand looked down at the floor. "I must leave, sensei."

"I know. I shall miss you, Robert-san. Thank you for
what you have done for me."

Sand looked up, slightly puzzled. "I did nothing for you,
sir. *You* helped me."

The old man smiled. "In you, Konuma-sensei lived again.
You brought my friend to me, if only for a little while.
You brought the past alive once more, for a short time.
You are *Samurai.*" His small wrinkled face quivered with
emotion, and his eyes grew bright with tears and memories. "Thank you," he whispered. He turned and was
gone from the doorway.

For a few seconds, Robert Sand stood in the silent,
empty room, his small suitcase in one hand. Then with

his fingers he gently brushed the tears beginning to fill his eyes and slowly walked from the room and into the dark hallway. His lips were pressed tightly together and his jaw trembled as he fought to hold back the tears.

CHAPTER 3

The Mission

"Valbonne sells guns to anybody," said William Baron Clarke, rolling up his white shirt sleeves, then reaching for the glass of bourbon and branch water on the small table near the long black couch. "Been harder than hell trying to get a picture on him, and for me that's sayin' something. I got a damn good file on the bastard, though."

It was a good one. The Baron had informants all over the world, in governments, in business, even in somebody's bed when need be. He paid them well, cash and tax-free, on time and steadily. In return, he wanted constant reports on anyone about to start worldwide trouble.

The information poured into him like water bursting through a broken dam. In the cellar of his sprawling Texas ranch house sitting in the middle of 1,250,000 acres of land were cases of microfilm, folders, files, photographs on thousands of people. Some were future trouble, others were immediate trouble.

Some of those on file were his contacts in different countries, on different levels of governments, businesses, in dozens of other areas. They collected the information and passed it on, and William Baron Clarke, not too many years out of the White House, remained one of the most informed men in the world on anything and anybody he wanted to know about.

What Clarke wanted to know was who was using his power to turn the world into more of a hell than God had made it. When he found out, that person became the mission. To the mission, the Baron brought information, power, money, influence. Robert Sand brought the heart, mind and skill of a Samurai warrior.

21

The Baron trusted no one he had once worked with. He'd learned that much from politics, where he'd made more than a few enemies. But he trusted the black Samurai, who because of his training with Master Konuma served moral right rather than the right made by might. It was Sand who had said, "Maybe we can't fight city hall, but we can burn it down." The Baron had laughed when he heard it, but his eyes were bright with its truth.

Now he sat in a gigantic penthouse suite in Tokyo's Imperial Hotel, drinking iced bourbon as though he were fighting 120-degree Texas heat.

"Damn Frenchman is a sumbitch, better believe it. He's selling guns to them Arab terrorists and hijackers. He's also selling guns to the Arabs in the Mideast. Jews too, if they got the money. He's selling to some bad-ass people over in Ireland, and at least five countries in South America. He's got dealings in Africa, too."

"Where is he getting his supply?" asked Sand, pouring himself a glass of water.

"Steals some. Buys some. Pays off guards, warehouse people. Kills if he has to. Picked up a lot of stuff in Vietnam, a lot of it sad to say from some greedy Americans and South Vietnamese. I just learned recently that he came across three goddam huge caches of weapons the Nazis had put away for a rainy day years ago. Found thousands of rifles, pistols, automatic weapons buried in the North African desert somewhere by Rommel. And he came across two piles of guns the Nazis hid in the Swiss mountains. In today's gun-happy world, all that stuff is worth a lot of money."

Sand drank the entire glass of water, then turned the empty glass around in his hand. "Too much of a coincidence those German guns turning up at the same time."

The Baron grinned, his tanned hawk-nosed face filling with creases and lines. "You *are* good, son, you goddam as hell are good. No coincidence at all. Somebody told Valbonne about those Nazi guns, and make no mistake about it, those guns shoot just as well as anything made yesterday. Hell, there's people out in the world killing each other with 60-, 70-year-old guns. Valbonne's getting ready for something big; that's one of the reasons why he learned about those guns."

Sand looked at the palms of his hands. The scars from

the chain were healing well. He thought of the old, gentle-looking man he left two hours ago. "A lot can happen in almost a month."

"Sorry to pull you out, but I guess I'd better make it short 'cause you got some travelin' to do. You're heading to Europe soon as possible. Valbonne's collecting people. That's right, people. He's collecting top German scientists from World War II, who worked on Germany's atomic bomb project. We stomped their butts before they could come up with the bomb, but they was only a hair from doin' it at the time. Some of their scientists are now working in America, some in Russia, some in Egypt. Valbonne's now got a handful of them working for him on something that—well, dammit, I find it hard to believe, but we got to look into it."

He stopped, then looked at Sand. "Hear me carefully, son, 'cause it ain't the bourbon talkin'. I've got reason to believe that the goddam Frenchman is buildin' his own atomic bomb."

Sand lifted his eyes to the Baron's face. "Why?"

"That's why I'm in Japan. You heard of a fella called Gozo Saraga?"

Sand knew the name. A Japanese shipowner, wealthy and militaristic, always calling for Japan to resume her days of military glory. He had read about Saraga for years and knew he was a potential troublemaker. "What's the connection between Saraga and Valbonne?"

"I been keepin' an eye on Valbonne since the beginning of the year, and sooner or later, I figured we got to stand in his way. Well, it's sooner. If he's buildin' that A-bomb, and that's what we both got to find out, then he plans to sell it to Saraga. I'm here because one of my informants close to Saraga says that Saraga has been talkin' about getting even for what America did to his family in World War II."

"They were in Nagasaki," said Sand. "Saraga's always saying that in his speeches, books and interviews. He's never forgotten their death. Claims he lost 29 members of his family in that atomic bombing. For him, I guess the atomic bomb falls every day."

"Better believe it. My informant, who I'll brief you on later, says that Saraga's feelin' happier than a pig in shit these days on account of he feels that he's gonna be

gettin' even soon. So far, there's not much to go on, but
—ah hell, Sand, I just might as well come out and say.
My man thinks Saraga's planning to A-bomb New York
City."

The black Samurai frowned, his eyes on the six-foot-
four Texan.

All he could say was, "You serious?"

"I didn't trust more news on this comin' in by letter,
tape or phone call. I came here to get it in person, and
when I got it, I grabbed hold of you. That's the Lord's
honest truth, on my sainted mother's grave. That yellow
bastard—'scuse me, son—plans to A-bomb New York,
with Valbonne's help. At least that's what it looks like,
and that's why I need you now."

Sand walked a few steps away from the Baron, turned,
and frowned. "Unbelievable. What's in it for Valbonne?"

"Same as he gets for gunrunning. Money, a lot of it.
A hundred million dollars is the figure being kicked
around."

Sand nodded his head several times. "Smart. He steals
an atomic bomb, or even tries to, and in seconds somebody comes down hard on his head. This way, he builds
his own and he doesn't have to worry about a knock on
the door. Smart."

"Too goddam smart, if you ask me. I've got some people near him too, and let me tell you they're scared shit-
less. Valbonne's a mean sumbitch, and other people's blood
is his hobby. He's got a bunch of hard cases workin' for
him. That's why it's been hard for me to get a pitcher of
him. Got a faded snapshot over on the desk, taken when
he was at an airport in Saigon a few years back. Check
it out before you leave. Watch out for one of his men
in particular, a full-blooded Apache named Mangas Salt.
He's big as a house, and is as tough as any of his redskin
ancestors."

Sand moved the corner of his mouth in a smile.
"Apache?"

"File on him over there, too. Born in Arizona, served
in Vietnam, six feet five of pure mean. Keeps the old
ways of his people and hates white men, particularly
American white men."

"Since when is that a personality defect?" asked the
black man.

"When you start castrating them or hanging them upside down over a fire and sit around watching until their skull splits open and their brains leak out. And that's just a few signs of his displeasure. He can be a helluva lot meaner 'n that."

"How did he and Valbonne get together?"

"Check the file. Salt deserted the Army in Vietnam, joined the Viet Cong, and fought against the American Army like his ancestors did a hundred years ago. Met Valbonne when the Frenchman was in North Vietnam on a huge gun deal. They been tight ever since. There's more to it than that, but it's all on paper. It's that bomb that grabs me by the cubes. Saraga's got a lot of money and a lot more hate for America. He's been the cause of a couple of riots just this past year, trying to get the Japanese government to go big on the military."

Sand knew that. There were those in Japan who wanted the old days of military power and expansion to return. But Saraga was different. He wanted that too, but he also wanted America pulled down to its knees. With his money and Valbonne's greed, anything was possible.

"Hell, son," said the Baron, reaching for the bourbon bottle, "Valbonne's sold everything you can think of. Rifles, pistols, bombs, planes, cannon, walkie talkies, you name it. But you think about it. He's got a big ego, and he would get a kick out of being the first man in history ever to sell an atomic bomb. Damn, he don't care what happens when he sells a piece of machinery that kills. If this stuff checks out, and something tells me it's gonna, Valbonne's got $100 million, plus some new guns his new German friends put him on to. And Saraga? He's set to get the thing an Oriental prizes a whole lot—revenge."

Sand understood. He'd gone almost around the world tracking the man who had slaughtered his beloved Master Konuma and his 22 Samurai brothers. When he found the man, he killed him. Yes, in the East revenge was an important emotion, and Sand knew enough about the Japanese to know that when they wanted revenge, nothing would stand in the way of getting it. Black as he was on the outside, inside Sand was Japanese to a very large degree.

Hadn't a famous Japanese writer spent much of his life praising the days when the military ran his country? And didn't that same writer kill himself as a means of protesting what he felt was his country's shame in not being more military? Yes, Saraga was a dangerous man, with money and power.

"When did your informant say Saraga plans to use the bomb?"

"Soon. Days, weeks. Couldn't learn much. Learned that the bomb's not here, so if it's anywhere it's in Europe. If Saraga didn't like to give speeches all the time, my man wouldn't have learned this much. Saraga would just as soon speak to one person as one hundred thousand."

"Those files—how complete are they?"

"As complete as money can make them. Things on Saraga, Valbonne, their people, their operations, and a separate folder on that goddam Apache. Watch him. He's a warrior from Geronimo's days, except that he's for real and John Wayne won't be around to help you."

"I want something else."

"What?"

"Every book you can get me on Apaches, people, customs, habits."

The Baron frowned. "You say so, son, but I don't see the sense of it. Got a file on him, I told you. It's right over there."

"That tells me what he's done. Doesn't tell me why. There's a reason why he's an Apache warrior still fighting like he was riding behind Geronimo. I want to know his mind, not just his record. My life's going to depend on knowing."

"You got it, son. I'll have the American embassy comb every English-language library in Tokyo. By the way, I'm givin' a speech tomorrow. That's my cover, another one of those goddam goodwill tours that give me heartburn and a case of the runs. Fortunately, this one only takes in three countries. Wife's with me. She's out spendin' money like they weren't gonna print any more. Women sure like to spend money."

"So does Saraga. Let's find out what he's getting for his $100 million. One thing I want understood. If Valbonne's making the bomb, one way to stop him or try to stop him is to *remove* some of the scientists he's got working for him."

"Remove?"

Sand smiled, then said softly, "It's a better word than 'kill.'"

"Your bat and your ball, son. You play your own

game. Just let me know what you need to play with. How you play the game is your own business. Remove, huh? Sheeit. Removin' Valbonne and Saraga is a service to God. Just you make sure of one thing."

"What?"

"Make sure that bad-ass Apache don't remove you."

CHAPTER 4

The Bomb

Valbonne combed his thinning brown hair sideways, patting it in place with small manicured fingers. Leaning his head slightly to the side, he smiled at his reflection. A square face, green eyes, wide mouth. Pleasant and friendly-looking. A small man, only five feet six inches tall. Forty-six years old, always well dressed, with impeccable manners.

"I want them all killed," he said, leaning his head to the left so that he could see the reflection of the huge Apache Indian sitting fully dressed on the large round white-fur-covered bed. The Indian—Mangas Salt—was silent, his dark-brown eyes watching the small man in front of the mirror. In six years of working for Valbonne, Salt had done a lot of killing. Now it was only a question of who, not how or why.

Valbonne pointed the silver comb toward the top of a small gold-painted table near his right. "This list has the names. Each person that could link a scientist to us, or who might tell interested parties that we've been collecting atomic materials. These people must be eliminated. Killing anyone earlier would have been ill-timed. Now we have what we need, scientific personnel, equipment and materials. So there's no chance that dead people will cause the living to become panicky and uncooperative."

Salt nodded. Valbonne was smart. Like a coyote hiding in shadows until he could creep up on a chicken. Smart as hell, that Valbonne.

"These names," said the Frenchman, turning around to look directly at Salt. "A couple here in Switzerland, some in France, England, the rest in America."

"What about the Jap, Saraga?" said Salt. "His people know."

"His problem. He's a tough man, our little Japanese friend. He'll do what's necessary to ensure silence until killing time. He's got more at stake than we do. Revenge is everything to him. Must avenge the family, that sort of thing. We're only in it for the money."

"One hundred million dollars. For that, we help him kill. Shit, must be over six million people in New York City now."

"You've been away from the States for some time, my Apache friend. *Over* seven million I believe, and the bomb we're constructing will send most of them to the heaven or hell they've earned by now."

"Still don't see why he doesn't steal one."

Valbonne smiled, his eyes warm and friendly. "My Apache friend, you are a master at killing. But you have much to learn about killing on a large scale. If Saraga steals an atomic bomb, assuming he is very, very lucky to even get it, someone will come looking for him immediately. They may take it back before he can use it. In any case, most of these bombs are too well guarded. He cannot build one without the right men, almost all of whom are working for me. Besides, he is such a public figure that his every move is news. Better for him to have nothing to do with such a project until the last possible moment."

"So we build it, sell it to him, and get the money."

"Ah, my friend, now, as you Americans put it, you are on the right track. We build the bomb, we sell it just as we would sell a pistol or a rifle. We get $100 million, much more than one would get for a pistol or a rifle. What Mr. Saraga does with the bomb is his affair. I make the coat, so to speak. I sell it. If you wish to eat the buttons or swallow the sleeves, that's your concern. It is nothing to me if he uses our product on America or Zambezia. I am sure you do not care about America, am I right?"

Salt's face hardened into intense cruelty and he spat on the gold-colored fur rug. "Shit. Damn country did nothing for me or any Indian but turn us into drunks, TB cases or goddam whores with syphilis. They put me in jail, forced me into the Army, then tried to throw my ass in the stockade. No, man, ain't nothing 'bout that place I'm hold-in' onto. *Pinda lick-o-yi*. They eat shit."

Pinda lick-o-yi. Apache for "white eyes."

Valbonne smiled. "Good. List is over here. Choose the men you want. Take some with you or pick them up when you get where you're going. Saraga will lend us some of his skilled Oriental muscle. Work alone when you feel you have to; it's all up to you. In matters like this, I trust you completely."

Salt nodded. He liked that about Valbonne. Trust. The Frenchman treated him with respect, paid him well, and never gave him a hard time. Sure Valbonne was white, but he was European white, not American white. That made a difference.

"You've got a week, maybe ten days at the most," said Valbonne. "We should finish construction of the bomb in twelve days, and with Saraga's shipping lines giving us a hand, we'll have our part of the bomb in New York five days after that."

Salt stood up, stretching his big arms toward the ceiling, his large body seeming to fill the luxurious gold-and-red bedroom in Valbonne's huge chalet. The chalet lay at the foot of mountains twenty miles outside of Geneva, Switzerland. "Damn smart, Mr. Valbonne. Making half the bomb here, the half with explosives in it, and making the trigger device in New York. No way anybody can grab it all and mess up your deal."

Nodding, the Frenchman accepted the compliment. "There's no way it can be done, Mangas. Most of all, it saves time. Two teams working on the bomb, with half of it being constructed next to the target, and the other half nearby where I can watch it day and night. That's the only part to smuggle into New York, because the trigger will already be there. Two teams, less time, more ef-ficiency. Yes, Mangas, it is a good plan."

"Should I be in Canada when Saraga's ship arrives? No sense letting the bomb be unloaded until he hands over the money."

"Good idea, Mangas. Partial payment is satisfying up to a point, but Saraga's insistence on holding back $50 million until the bomb lands in Canada is a good business practice for him, not for me. You and your men be there. I leave it to you to make sure Mr. Saraga settles his bill before the bomb leaves the ship and is loaded on a truck."

"If he doesn't have the money, he doesn't get the merchandise. Don't worry, Mr. Valbonne, I'll collect."

Valbonne walked over to Salt, and patting a huge bicep said, "I'm not worried, Mangas. You'll be there, that will be enough. Remember, though, Mr. Saraga will have some of his own men with him, and they are well trained in the martial arts. They may be the same men who'll be working with you to eliminate the men on that list. Saraga's agreed with me that his men take orders from you. You may have to enforce that, but I can't see the problem there."

"Neither can I."

"Good. It's our chance to write history, playing a part in the first bombing of an American city. You're to go to France tomorrow. Leave the people in Switzerland to last; I don't want news of their deaths to upset those working on the bomb. France first, then England. Switzerland, then New York. From there, you go to Canada and collect our final payment from Mr. Saraga. You'll be in touch with me all the time, and we'll plan on a meeting here before you go to America. Now, I have a surprise for you."

Smiling, the Frenchman turned and hurried across the gold carpet, opening the bedroom door and speaking softly in French. Stepping aside, he continued to smile as three women walked by him and into the bedroom. Their heads turned right then left, eyes wide with wonder at the large room luxuriously decorated all in gold. "Ooo la la," said a tall, thin blonde, sucking on her little finger. "I like this place."

A red-haired English girl, nineteen, with a round freckled face, said, "You could land a plane in this room. Look, Maria, the bloody place is gold from top to bottom."

Looking at Salt, Maria, a 23-year-old Italian with huge breasts and jet-black hair, wrinkled her long nose and said, "This one is not gold, unless he is hiding it somewhere." The other two women turned their faces toward Salt.

"Heaven help us," said Rachel, the English girl, her eyes moving up and down the huge Indian as though he were a tourist attraction in a strange country. The three were prostitutes, hired for the night at $1,000 each.

"My surprise," said Valbonne, smiling at Salt. "A going-away present. Enjoy yourself, my friend." He left the room, closing the door behind him.

Salt leaned his large head back, his dark-brown eyes moving from woman to woman, his coarse black hair catching the lights from the ceiling. Maria, her pink tongue wetting her lips, moved toward Salt, her hands reaching out to him and fondling his groin. Her eyes brightened and she laughed, "This one, he's got enough down there to choke a giraffe."

The women moved toward him, giggling, hands caressing his body, fingers unbuckling his belt, sliding into the warmth of his groin. Rachel said, "Lord, I haven't seen one this size since that African from the embassy made me so sore I was bowlegged for a month."

"Loving every minute of it, too," said the thin Norwegian blonde, whose name was Nora. "Well, Mr. Apache Indian, you may be a big man, but we intend to cut you down to our size."

Salt's mouth moved in a cruel sneer, and he took off his red shirt, the muscles of his chest and shoulders pushing up hard under the skin.

Maria licked her lips, her hands behind her neck unzippering her tightly fitting black wool dress. She wore nothing under it. Her breasts, large and tanned, the light-brown nipples hard with sex, hung free. Stepping from the dress, she pushed the two other women aside and fell to her knees in front of Salt, a low moan crawling from her throat.

Her hands reached into his opened fly, filling her fingers with his hardened flesh, and she opened her mouth.

Behind her, the other two prostitutes quickly stripped themselves naked and stepped toward Salt.

Valbonne watched, his eyes bright in the darkness of the small room on the other side of the mirror. His mouth widened in a smile of satisfaction, and his chest and stomach heaved with his deep breathing. Both of his hands moved up and down his own thighs, and in the darkness, his breathing grew louder.

He leaned closer to the mirror.

In a small, dirty-yellow brick house 40 miles outside of Paris, Robert Sand sat facing a closed door, the bright-orange sunset at his back, his dark-blue raincoat folded across his muscular thighs. He listened quietly as Brian Turpin, a 55-year-old Englishman with a bald head and puffs of gray hair around his ears, talked and sipped a warm gin and tonic.

Turpin, a forger and counterfeiter, squinted his eyes against the sun, his left hand trying to shade his face. "Bloody window. Been meaning to get some curtains in this room. Where was I? Oh yes. This time Valbonne wanted a job done in a bleedin' hurry. Two passports, one Swiss, the other American, and it's a rush. I'm to drop everything and concentrate on these passports, see, and all the while, he's got a couple of his boys hangin' around me place to see that I don't go out and nobody else comes in. Oh, he pays me well. So does your Mr. Clarke."

Sand nodded, his handsome face relaxed, his eyes staring at the red-faced Englishman.

"Now I ain't dumb, see, I knows somethin's happenin'. Like both of the men what wants the passports are here watchin'. They don't speak, but get this, they both have Egyptian newspapers, cigarettes, and the clothes they're wearin' look like somethin' a camel pissed on. Damn Egyptians never could dress right. Now both these men speak German to each other. Both are old, in their sixties, maybe seventies. Names I get are Hans Richter for the Swiss passport, Jan Klaus for the American."

"That one was Dutch," said Sand.

"Indeed sir, indeed. Both looked like college professors, you know that mixed-up, couldn't-find-their-asses-with-both-hands look. I know the job's for Valbonne 'cause he's sent his flunky Pierre Roth to watch me. Good money, but I figured I might as well tell the Baron about it, and I did."

Sand nodded.

Turpin said, "The Baron, he sure thinks a lot of you. Told me to give you what you want or he'd slice off what little I've got hangin' between me legs." He laughed, closing his eyes against the sun, opening his mouth of rotten teeth and swallowing more warm gin.

A corner of Sand's mouth moved in a smile. He looked around the room piled high with papers, faded photographs, newspapers, broken pens, and bottles of ink. They were in a small room on the ground floor of the dirty, cluttered house. From the other side of the closed door, sounds of a man's voice singing in French came over a radio. A glass fell to the floor and broke.

"Damn Frenchwoman," said Turpin. "Fat as a pregnant

elephant, ugly as a worm's asshole, but she can cook like an angel. Thank God I only have to screw her once a month. Ugh!" He made a face and finished his warm gin. Wiping an ink-stained hand across his wet lips, he said, "You ought to look up Racine. George Racine. He's the one what flew them here from Spain." He pronounced it "spine."

"How do you know?"

Turpin grinned, his black, broken teeth bright with spit. "In our business, everybody knows everybody. Besides, while he was here Roth mentioned Racine's name. From that point it was easy. What's the Baron so interested in two old doddering Germans for? If you ask me—"

A woman screamed, high, shrill, the sound as piercing as an icepick jammed into an eardrum. Sounds of breaking glass, then the heavy thump of feet racing toward Sand and the Englishman. Brian's mouth dropped open and he turned in his chair, "Here now, what's—"

The door burst open, slamming hard against the wall, sending papers flying and a framed copy of an antique map crashing to the floor. A squat muscular Japanese with a thick black mustache stood crouching in the doorway, both arms crossed to push away the sun suddenly in his face.

Another Japanese pushed past him, arm held high, then with a swift move, he brought the arm down, smashing his weapon, a nunchaku, across the head of the Englishman.

Nunchaku. Two ten-inch-long sticks joined by a one-foot leather thong. Long used in the Far East as a deadly weapon. Used to strike or choke a man. Used to cripple or smash him anywhere on his body. Nunchaku. Now outlawed in many countries around the world.

Blood slid across Turpin's pink bald skull and he tumbled from the chair, scattering papers and black ink before him. As the Japanese moved closer to the bleeding man now on the floor, the squat mustached Japanese yelled, then charged Sand.

The sun-blinded attacker had hesitated in the doorway, giving the black Samurai precious seconds. Neither the black man nor the Japanese rushing toward him had weapons. Sand, however, had the raincoat and the chair he was sitting on.

Quickly leaping up sideways from the chair, he yanked

it forward with his left hand, spinning his body in place
to add more strength to the move. The chair rolled awkwardly but swiftly to meet the attacker, hitting him
between knees and ankle. He stumbled, going toward the
floor, his left arm out stiff to break his fall.

Yelling "Kiaaai!" Sand lifted his own left knee high, then
shot the leg out as far as it would go in a powerful
thrust kick, aiming downward at the attacker's head. His
foot tore into the man's face, smashing his nose, snapping
his head backward. The man went down and didn't move.

From the corner of his eye, Sand saw the motion. The
attacker with the deadly nunchaku looked up from the
Englishman bleeding on the paper-covered floor, and
leaped toward Sand, the weapon held high for striking.
With split-second timing, the black Samurai waited until
the distance narrowed between them, then tossed the raincoat over the man's head.

Without stopping, Sand followed his own motion, closing the distance between them and driving a powerful elbow smash to the man's covered head. He heard the
man's muffled cry under the coat. As the man staggered backward, both arms wide for balance, Sand closed
the distance once more and front-kicked the man in the
balls, driving him through the doorway, out into the hall
and hard into the opposite wall.

As the man slid down the wall into a sitting position,
his head still covered by the dark blue raincoat, Sand heard
more footsteps running along the corridor.

Quickly stepping forward, he bent over and picked up
the nunchaku, remaining crouched, one hand tightly gripping one of the ten-inch wooden sticks. The handle had
been wrapped in black tape for a secure grip and was
still wet with the sweat of the man who had just dropped
it.

Sand's face was grim, his eyes intense on the open doorway. The footsteps slowed, then a man appeared in the
doorway, his back almost to Sand. Japanese. One of the attackers. Bending over, a small Japanese pistol in his right
hand, he reached out to pull the raincoat off the man
now unconscious and sitting against the wall.

In seconds, he'd turn, see the black Samurai, and start
shooting.

With instincts sharpened in years of brutal, demanding
Samurai training, Sand snapped his wrist, sending the other

wooden stick spinning in the air toward himself. Now he gripped both handles. Without hesitation, his powerful arm came back, then forward, and the nunchaku sped through the air toward the attacker crouching over the unconscious man covered by the blue raincoat, and Sand rushed forward.

The raincoat slid off, revealing the unconscious Japanese's bleeding face. Swiftly, the crouching attacker turned, bringing his gun hand up. Then both hands flew quickly to his face in a vain attempt to knock the wooden weapon aside. It hit his forehead, and he staggered to his right, falling to one knee.

Yelling at the top of his voice, a hoarse animal cry of warriors over thousands of years, the black Samurai leaped high into the air, his feet tightly under him; then, still in midair, he quickly extended his right leg as far out as it could go, throwing all of his power into the kick, driving the tensed foot deep into the gunman's left temple.

The gunman landed on his back, out cold, his long black hair covering his face, blood creeping from beneath the hair. Quickly, Sand scooped up the gun and turned toward the direction the men had come from. There was no sound in front of the house. Then, to his right, a man moaned. Turpin.

In less than two minutes, Sand had checked both the ground floor and the top floor. There were no more attackers. The fat woman was dead, lying on her side in the kitchen like a beached whale, her neck circled by a deadly purple necklace, the marks where the leather thong of the nunchaku had choked her to death.

Turpin crouched over her, his blood-covered face looking suddenly years older. His hand reached out to her, touching her thin, dyed black hair. Softly he said, "Silly old cow." His lips trembled and his bloodshot eyes were bright with tears. "Silly old cow," he muttered again and again.

Sand stood looking down at the Englishman and the dead fat woman. "You can't stay here. Valbonne sent these men to kill you. You know too much."

Turpin stared at the dead woman, his watery eyes on her but unseeing. His voice was husky in his throat. "Valbonne. Valbonne."

Sand leaned over, his hand lifting Turpin to his feet. "Racine's address. Quickly. Where is it?"

Turpin's lips moved, but no sound came out. Sand gripped both of the man's shoulders, his brown eyes intense on Turpin's face. "Racine. His life's in danger. His address. Now!" His fingers dug into the Englishman's flabby shoulders.

An hour later, Sand stood in the cellar of Racine's farmhouse, staring at the airplane pilot. The woman—she was either his wife or his girl friend—had died quickly. She had been strangled, and her body lay fully clothed at the foot of the old wooden stairs.

Racine was a different matter.

Sand's face, tense and grim, wrinkled with the sickening smell.

Racine hung upside down from the ceiling, feet tied together and tightly roped to a thick brown wooden beam. His head hung down over what had been a small fire. Thin wisps of gray smoke curled upward from the stone floor. Both hands were tied behind his back. The fire had burned his head, neck and shoulders, turning the flesh a bloody and ugly black.

The fire had also made his skull swell, then burst open like an egg flattened by a truck. The cellar was filled with the sickening odor of charred flesh, and the pink ooze that had been Racine's brains lay in a sticky mess near the remains of the fire.

He had died the Apache way.

Sand turned, hurrying up the stairs and out into the cold and increasing darkness. Again and again he took deep breaths, anxious to drive the smell of burning flesh from his mind and body.

Valbonne and his Apache Indian Mangas Salt were involved in something serious enough to kill people for. The Japanese attackers at Turpin's house meant that Saraga was involved, too.

It added up to one thing. The Baron's worst fears were confirmed.

CHAPTER 5

Saraga

Gozo Saraga, gray hair cropped close to his skull, knelt alone in the quiet room, thinking of revenge.

Others talked of it. He, Saraga, would do it.

Revenge.

Narrowing his eyes, he stared at the flickering orange-and-blue flames dancing on top of the two white candles. A black glass bowl of sweet-smelling incense sent blue smoke curling slowly up from the floor toward the ceiling. Sitting back on his heels, his hands resting palms down on his thighs, he breathed deeply.

Many Japanese had shaken with hatred for America, spitting at the mention of her name, for what had been done to Japan in World War II. *But no Japanese had done what had to be done.* The 55-year-old Japanese shipping magnate closed his eyes entirely, relaxing his mind, his body.

Revenge. A flame roaring within him, never going out.

Twenty-nine years ago. In 1945 the Americans had dropped an atomic bomb on Nagasaki, killing 36,000 Japanese and mutilating almost 40,000 more. Saraga had been a thin, sickly 26-year-old American prisoner of war on Okinawa. Like many Japanese soldiers, he had fought tenaciously, giving up only when there was no ammunition to fight with and no rats and lizards to eat.

There had been nothing for him to do when he had heard the news of the bombing, except to grip the barbed-wire fence of the prison camp tightly until the blood oozed from between his pain-filled fingers.

Weeks later, he returned to Japan and learned that his mother, father and three sisters were among 29 relatives killed in the bombing. Twenty-nine people he had loved intensely, killed by an American atomic bomb. An old woman who had known his mother, and who had been on a visit miles away that day, had said to him, "I wanted to see my son Yaka, the one who had been your comrade in school. Well, I traveled ten days on foot because there was no transportation at that time. The Americans, you know, they had killed us from the skies. I managed to get to the hospital that had been set up some miles away from Nagasaki. We were forbidden to go near the town because of radiation. I saw my son, what was left of him. He died as I was coming down the hospital corridor to see him.

"On the way out, I stopped to see if I knew anyone else there. Your mother, Gozo, your mother. She screamed and screamed and I watched her. The bleeding skin was sliding from her flesh as though she were removing clothing. The white of her skull could be seen, and her eyes had melted. Your mother, she screamed so much. I am sorry."

He vowed revenge on the spot. One year of his life was dedicated to each of the 29 relatives. At the end of 29 years, he would avenge them. He would strike back at the despised nation that had ripped life from them and all love from him.

Wealth and work was now his life. A wife and family would have been a drain on his energy and time, so he had sought neither. He took a woman when he needed her, rarely remembering her name. At the beginning of the 29th year, he had walked into this quiet, private room in his sprawling, well-guarded home, fallen to his knees, and wept.

Soon. Soon he would avenge them. Twenty-nine years after 1945.

1974 was the year he would set off an atomic bomb in New York City, the most populated city in America. He was one of the wealthiest men in Japan, the owner of dozens of cargo ships, with thousands of people working for him. None of that mattered.

What mattered was the year 1974, time to avenge those he had been powerless to save 29 years ago.

In the quiet, candlelit room, the squat, gray-haired Japanese sat quietly on his heels and thought of bleeding flesh peeling silently from his mother's skull.

"Shit," said the Baron. "We're in it now, up to the whole eyeball." His Texas drawl came over the static-filled telephone connection, his voice packed with disgust and apprehension. He was in Seoul, Korea. Sand was in Paris.

"Tell you something, son. It ain't enough to go 'round tellin' people 'bout our Japanese friend's plans for the big city. He's the type to keep on tryin' until somethin' happens to whoever or whatever he's got a hatred for. We got to stop him, see that he doesn't go to bat again. Turpin, you got him stashed?"

"Yes," said Sand, not wanting to say too much over the phone.

The Baron understood. Sand could almost see the tan Texan nodding approval. "That's your department, son. See what else you can squeeze outta him. Right now, I'm visiting the president of this here country I once gave $200,000,000 to in one day. Callin' you on an embassy phone supposedly untapped, but you never can tell these days."

Sand's face was grim. "No choice. I wanted you to know as soon as possible. Now you know who to go after. Move in on the Japanese shipping man. See if you can buy somebody close to him."

"No problem," drawled the Texan. "Money does the loudest talkin'. 'Tween that and me knowin' where the bodies are buried, I'll get closer to him than a pimple on his butt."

"Next, check out Egypt. Find out who left recently."

"I understand. Oh, before I forget, there'll be a cable waitin' for you at your hotel with a name. That's your Paris contact for whatever you might need. As usual, I'm shellin' out big money for services rendered, so don't be afraid to make demands. Now that I know where we got to go, I'm coming down hard on anybody who's got a song to sing."

The full might of the Baron's wealth and power was in motion, aimed at Saraga, Valbonne and anyone who lately might have gone into a deadly line of work. The Baron had muscle, and knew how to use it.

Sand said, "You'll hear from me later."

"Watch out for our friend from Arizona, son. He plays with matches."

Sand hung up.

The Apache way of killing.

Salt's strong fingers knotted an end of the long brown rawhide strip around the perspiring neck of Marcel Vain, a stocky, red-faced French laboratory technician. Swiftly, the other end was lashed around Vain's ankles. Vain lay on his side, white adhesive tape across his thick lips, his watery blue eyes bulging in fear. Blood covered the rawhide cutting into his wrists.

To ease the stiffness and cramps gnawing at his legs, Vain moved his legs forward. Suddenly, his eyes bulged even more. The slight movement had cut off some of his air. Legs or head—to move either was to choke himself to death. His face turned redder as he fought for air.

Now, the huge Apache stood looking down at the perspiring frightened man who had been paid well to get a small quantity of uranium for Valbonne. Salt's cruel face, the slash of white paint under both eyes and across the bridge of his nose, turned from the man tied with rawhide on the floor to an opened bottle of red wine on a tiny green table in Vain's small apartment.

In seconds, the bare-chested Indian held the half-filled bottle of wine in his large fist. Leaning over Vain, Salt carefully poured red wine over the rawhide. First at the stocky Frenchman's throat, the wine blending into Marcel Vain's tears.

Then over the bound wrists and ankles.

Soon the rawhide would dry and shrink, biting deep into Vain's flesh. Soon it would choke him to death, if his struggling didn't strangle him first. The Apache way of killing.

Sitting on the bare wooden floor of the small apartment, Mangas Salt crossed his legs, took a deep breath, then relaxed, his hard eyes on the man who would be dead in minutes.

Salt watched Marcel Vain yield to panic. As the wine-soaked rawhide around his neck began to shrink, the Frenchman leaned his head backward, desperately trying to ease the pressure. His heart pumped furiously, each beat seeming to touch his ribs. Wine had stained the Frenchman's white shirt and had left dark wet spots on his blue pants.

The Apache watched, his mind traveling back. . . .

Arizona.

He had been born Juan José Mangas Salt, a Mimbreño

Apache. The name Mangas had been for Mangas Coloradas, one of the fierce Apache chiefs of the nineteenth
century, a human tiger, in the tradition of Geronimo,
Cochise, Vittorio, Ulzana, Ponce. All of these men had
been fighters, each cunning, cruel and determined against
the blue-coat soldiers with their long knives, against the
pinda lick-o-yi, the white eyes who swallowed up Indian
land like a snake swallowing up a mouse.

Both Mangas Coloradas, called Red Shirt or Red Sleeves,
and Juan José Mangas Salt had been big men, each well
over six feet tall. Juan José had grown up feeling apart
from other modern Apaches who lived on the reservation
near Nogales, got TB, got drunk, and died.

The Indian version of white man's school bored him.
He wanted to learn of the old days when Apaches killed
whites and didn't have to step off the sidewalk when
drunken white cowboys drove pick-up trucks in town for
Saturday drinking and whoring.

The old days. When Apaches were warriors racing the
wind on horses, traveling 100 miles a day over green land
juicy with water and black with buffalo herds. Today, the
land was dry, raped by whites the same way they had
raped Indian women.

Twentieth-century whites hated the Apaches as much
as nineteenth-century whites ever had. And Mangas Salt—
he had stopped using his first two names—hated twentieth-
century American whites with an intensity surpassing their
hate for him.

At eighteen, six feet four, weighing 200 pounds, he had
gone into an all-white café in town on a Saturday night,
feeling the eyes on him, hearing the drawled whispers of
"redhide nigger" follow him up to the scarred wooden
bar. When the white bartender refused him whiskey,
hands hidden under the bar and tightly gripping a sawed-
off pool cue, Salt had been ready. The bartender had said,
"Fuckin' injun—" and got no further.

Salt's fist tore into his throat, crushing the larynx. Chairs
scraped against the bar's wooden floor, animal cries roared
from men's throats as they rushed forward, eager to
grind their bootheels into the muscular Indian youth's
face.

Salt turned to face them.

His eyes gleamed brightly in the light of the small, rundown bar, as his hand slid inside his red shirt and came

out with the Bowie knife, its long, curved blade razor-sharpened on both sides, the steel bright under yellow lights.

Crouching, he opened his mouth and let out an ancient Apache warcry the old drunken men of his tribe had taught him.

As the highpitched sound came from his throat, he rushed forward to meet them.

Later, the judge had said, "You're lucky—no one died," before sentencing him to two years in jail. No one had died. But five white men would remember that night. One lost three fingers on his right hand, another's lung was pierced so badly it had to be removed. One man lost an eye, while another's face looked as though a crazed bear had clawed it.

The bartender would spend the rest of his life speaking only in a horrible whisper.

In prison, Mangas had fought. He fought the vicious homosexuals who carried knives made from sharpened teaspoons. He fought the racists—white and black—who challenged him and tried to use him. He fought the prison drug peddlers. Until the prison population got the message and paid him the ultimate tribute. They left him alone.

Once when he had been put in solitary for fighting, he had survived the Apache way. He found a rusty nail on the floor of his cell. With strong teeth, he bit as much of the rust from the nail as he could, cleaning it with his spit and his tongue.

He waited awhile to be sure. But he knew. There would be no food, no water for him until the tough warden decided there would be. The food and water he might have gotten could easily have been withheld from him by guards paid off by convicts anxious to revenge themselves against the giant Apache.

In the darkness and loneliness of his filthy cell, Salt grinned. Apache. He had listened to the drunken old men of his tribe tell stories they had heard from fathers and grandfathers, stories passed down from generation to generation, because the white man did not keep Apache history except to study him as though he were a bug.

Survival. Apache warriors survived.

Gripping the nail in the fingers of his right hand, he scraped it against a vein in his left wrist until he drew blood. Five times a day he sucked his own blood. He did this for the four days he was given no food or water.

And his mind helped him. He dreamed of Geronimo and Mangas Coloradas, of how Apache warriors once covered 75 miles on foot across desert with American soldiers seeking to kill them, of how Apache scalps were collected by whites and sold to Mexicans for $100 each, $50 for women, $25 for children. He used hate to stay alive. He thought of the skin being peeled from the naked bodies of dead Apaches and used to make boots for hated bluecoated Army officers, of breasts sliced from Apache women to make tobacco pouches for white men, of four-teen-year-old Apache girls kidnapped and forced to work in white men's whorehouses. White man's conquest.

His hate and his Apache blood kept him alive. And when he heard the key turn in the solid steel door of his cell, he struggled to his feet, standing with his legs wide apart, his bright eyes burning into the armed guards pointing shotguns at him.

Apache.

They set the bread and water down, spilling some of the water in their haste to leave. He waited until the door closed and the key turned before moving to the food. He felt no shame at licking the water from the floor. Apache warriors must survive.

Later, he learned that white man's politics are still used against the Apache of today as they were 100 years ago. When his jail term was up, it was white man's political pressure that forced him directly into the Army under threat of more jail.

He was placed in an infantry unit, one of the first to be shipped to Vietnam as "dumb fuckin' targets." He fought well, always keeping to himself, going "point" on patrol, the first man to meet the enemy.

But he could never forget he was an Apache in a white man's world. Soldiers around him were careful never to tease him about being an Apache. He never said a word about it. It was just understood.

But an officer, a captain fresh from the States, drank too much to celebrate his new post and made the mistake of stopping Salt on a Saigon street and ordering him to do a war dance. "That's an order, mister," the drunken, blond-haired captain had said, "and you had better move your red ass in rhythm or you'll end up in barbed-wire city."

Sheeit, goin' to the stockade for this? Salt turned to walk away, when he felt his arm grabbed, the flesh pinched painfully.

When he turned, he saw the .45 in the drunken captain's hand. "Fuckin' red nigger, maybe if I *made* you dance, you just might start to move your ass, I betcha that, ol' buddy."

He had the gun pointed down at Salt's feet like some bad Western movie. But none of the men that night were living a movie. Neither the drunken captain nor the two drunken, grinning officers with him were in a movie.

Swiftly, Sand grabbed the gun hand, turning it back into the captain's belly. When the gun roared, the powerful pistol lifted the man off his feet and into the air, then down on the concrete, writhing side to side in pain. The Apache had seen enough death to know the officer didn't have any more time left on earth than he could hold in his hand.

"Your ass!" screamed a thin lieutenant, his sparse mustache wet with spit. Pointing to Salt, he screamed again. "Your ass, Indian! We'll see you never take another breath of free air in your damn life."

Sheeit. White man's justice. Throwing an Apache in prison was like breaking all four legs on a fast young horse. Prison. It had killed so many of the warrior chiefs. And Mangas Coloradas, the fierce Red Sleeves, he had been tricked into surrendering and then killed while lying on the cold ground in a United States military post, huddled under a thin blanket near a campfire.

Without warning, soldiers had jabbed the great old chief with heated bayonets, and when he protested and tried to crawl away, the soldiers had emptied their guns into him. Afterward, Mangas Coloradas had been scalped and his head cut off.

That night in Saigon, Salt vowed on the spot. No more prison. Never.

Turning, he had fled into the night.

A week later, he had made contact with Viet Cong spies in Saigon and moved from his hiding place north with them.

Two weeks later, he fought with them against the Americans. He had no conscience on this matter. No doubts, no hesitation. It was the Apache tradition to fight the Americans. It had been inevitable for Mangas Salt to do so.

He had been fighting with them two years when he met Valbonne. Both men were in Hanoi, Salt as the second-in-command to an important Viet Cong unit seeking guns, Valbonne to personally conclude a $5 million arms deal with Hanoi.

They had talked, and then Valbonne had listened. He was attracted and amused by the Apache, who was no movie Indian but a real live weapon. That was it. The Apache was a weapon and Valbonne dealt in weapons. What started as a whim developed into genuine interest. During the five days Valbonne was in Hanoi, he talked with the Apache as much as time would allow.

Salt was looking for a change of scenery. The Vietnam war would end one day. Valbonne offered him a change, plus money, more money than Salt had ever thought he could make. To earn it, Salt had to continue doing what he was doing, except that from now on, he did it for Valbonne. Bodyguard, courier for money or messages, avenger for any doublecross.

They shook hands, Valbonne's small white fingers lost in the large brown fist of the Apache. Salt liked him. Valbonne was out for money and he didn't care how he got it. He served no one but himself, and he had no moral code other than survival. The Apache understood all this. Above all, Valbonne treated Salt with respect.

The Apache liked that. Valbonne seemed interested in Apache life, as many Europeans were, and he listened respectfully to the old stories and to the Apache's bitterness. If Salt missed America, he didn't show it. There was nothing for him there but an old drunken father who sometimes forgot where Salt's mother was buried.

America was nothing to him. All it had given any Apache was a past crammed with bloodshed.

In Vietnam he had seen and smelled death. At times he could taste it. In the jungles, in small, stinking villages, in rice paddies. It had made him more and more determined to live the rest of his life as what he might have been years ago. As an Apache warrior.

He would live that way, and if he had to he would die that way.

Now he sat on the floor watching Marcel Vain's swollen red face.

Calmly, as though watching a puppy at play, Salt stared at the man being choked to death by the shrinking rawhide covered in blood and wine.

Salt felt no more emotion over this than if he had been staring at a blank wall.

CHAPTER 6

Airport Attack

Robert Sand laid the Colt .45 ACP Commander on his lap, feeling the heavy metal of the powerful handgun pressing against his black leatherclad thighs. He sat in the front seat of a gray Citroen parked in darkness at the edge of an abandoned small airfield 40 miles north of Paris. Charles Clary, a 35-year-old Frenchman with thick glasses and a nose flat from being broken too many times, sat beside him, strong fingers drumming on the hard brown plastic steering wheel.

Clary dealt in stolen goods, selling and receiving. He spoke five languages, had once fought 40 bouts as a middleweight boxer, and knew the black market of Europe. Clary was well paid by the Baron for information on people who stole anything big in Europe.

He was Sand's Paris contact.

Both men stared straight ahead at the darkened small hangar and empty airfield.

"Oui, Robert," he said. "As I told you, this is not much of an airfield. German officers used it during the war for quick weekend trips to other cities with their wives or French girl friends. Then it was used for pleasure, only small planes, nothing big. Bigger strips were all filled with planes of war. The man we wait for uses this one for his business trips."

The man they waited for was Pierre Monbouque, who specialized in illegal flying jobs, no questions asked.

Touching the gun lying in his lap, Sand said, "Thanks for this."

Clary said, "My pleasure. Your friend the Baron makes it possible for me to own an excellent collection of rare books. Unlike many of my comrades, I am not dependent upon crime to pay my bills. The American President has given me independence."

"Monbouque seems to be independent, too."

"Ah, yes. Mr. M., as we call him. In our business, everybody knows everybody else. When an item of value is stolen or smuggled, we all learn about it because some of us may want to buy it. Money is made on everything stolen, no matter where it happens. A few weeks ago, I offered Mr. M. a job. He said no. Told me he had a job to do for Valbonne in England. Two days after he tells me that, a laboratory blows up outside Cambridge, in England."

Sand nodded. "The British do some atomic work there."

"Correct, my friend. The lab blew up, two men were killed, and supposedly some atomic materials were destroyed. But I hear differently. I hear that Valbonne was involved, that the explosion was no accident. People today are ready to buy armaments of any kind, guns, bombs, even a slingshot if it kills. But we in the black market were told that the material in that laboratory was *not* for sale, that Valbonne already had it."

Sand smoothed the sleeves of his tight-fitting leather jacket, then shifted to stretch his legs in front of him. "Mr. M. plus Racine. One flies in atomic material, the other flies in atomic manpower. Turpin makes passports. Racine is dead, Turpin was almost killed but is alive and drinking. While Mr. M. is still missing."

"Patience, my American friend. He is returning from a job, I am told. He flew perfume to Scotland yesterday and will return tonight, my source tells me."

"Who is your source?"

"His sister. We live together."

Sand smiled at the flat-nosed Frenchman who collected rare books and made his living selling stolen goods. "His sister?"

"*Oui.*"

Then they heard it.

A car scraping slowly along the dirt road behind them, motor coughing, pale-yellow headlights sliding out of the darkness, flashing brightly between trees, then moving on. Sand and Clary were off the road, well hidden. The black Samurai, a careful man, had insisted on being at the airfield an hour and a half before the plane was due to land. Clary's hand was inside his camel's-hair overcoat, fingers clutching a 9mm M1950 pistol, strongest handgun made in France.

Whoever it is doesn't know the road too well, thought the black Samurai. He whispered to Clary, "Valbonne's men. Japanese or some Europeans. If the Indian's with them, be careful." He had told Clary about Salt and about the judo-karate killers on loan to Valbonne from Saraga. Clary had smiled, then chuckled as he listened to Sand speak about the Apache. He stopped laughing when Sand told him about Racine's brains drying out on the cold stone floor of a French farmhouse.

The car passed them, rolling down a slight incline, then across the broken, ill-kept concrete runway and into the small hangar. The engine roared, then was cut. The headlights stayed on as four men got out of the car, two with flashlights.

Even in the darkness and from a distance, Sand saw that the huge Apache Salt was not with them. Sand had his hand on the doorknob ready to open the wide door of the Citroen when he heard the plane in the air. "Damn!" he said aloud.

Ducking his head and looking up at the sky through the front windshield, Clary said, "He flies low to avoid detection. He is quick, our Mr. M. He will circle once, then land. He does not need any lights. His sister says he uses landmarks, trees, rocks, anything. He is one hell of a pilot, our Mr. M. He can land a plane in your bedroom and not disturb your sleep."

Sand's mind raced swiftly. He had planned to get to the hangar, take out Valbonne's men, then wait with Clary to grab Monbouque the instant his plane touched down on the runway. Now the plane would be landing at the same time Sand would be stalking the killers. He had counted on having time. Now there would be no time. Everything had to be done quickly. He had to risk being seen by the plane.

"It's getting harder, but we're going ahead anyway. I'm going to the hangar, you go for the plane. Except there's no time to be clever. I want you to crash into the plane."

Clary frowned, his face twisted in a combination of doubt, fear, reluctance.

"I can't risk having him get away," said Sand. "I need anything that can lead me to Valbonne's atomic bomb.

Nothing fancy. Go for the tail, a wheel, anything to make sure that plane doesn't get off the ground."

The flat-nosed Frenchman licked his lips, his hands gripping the wheel, opening, then gripping it again. "Robert, I—"

"Five thousand dollars. Hit the plane, stop it anyway you can, and there's 5,000 American dollars for you. The Baron's told you about me; you know I mean what I say. I promise you the money tomorrow."

Clary's face relaxed by inches, his eyes staring straight ahead. The sound of the plane grew louder. His voice was a husky, harsh whisper. "Yes! Yes!"

"Good." Sand pulled a black ski mask from inside his black leather jacket, slipping it over his head. Quickly he adjusted the slits around his eyes and mouth.

Seconds later he slipped from the car and blended into the darkness. The roar of the plane grew louder.

Pierre Monbouque pulled back hard on the throttle, clearing the two darkened trees by less than six feet, the wind from his two propellers flattening green and yellow leaves in the direction he was heading. In the darkness, he flew like an owl, using almost hidden landmarks as though they were beacons. The harsh white light from the nose of his plane turned the ill-kept runway in front of him a gray-white. Blackness was on both sides of him, as though he had landed inside a giant mine shaft, with only the light on his cap to guide him.

His concentration was entirely on landing the plane, and he heard nothing over the roar of the powerful engine.

Releasing his brake, Clary rolled down the incline, using no lights, no motor, rolling onto the runway in the darkness, directly for the small plane floating down toward him. Then—

He gunned the motor into action, snapping on the ignition, his foot jamming the accelerator into the floor, the car roaring to life, jumping, jerking, then speeding toward the small plane now feet from the runway. Sharply turning the wheel to the right, Clary moved the car out of the path of the oncoming plane, moving away from it.

Then he turned the car in a half circle, aiming it toward the path of the plane, toward a now-empty spot where he and the plane would meet in seconds.

The small plane touched down, its wheels screeching

on the cracked, broken cement, portions of the runway pushed upward out of place by decay.

A tall Frenchman standing in the darkness of the hangar took the cigarette from his mouth, leaning his head forward, straining to see what his ears may have heard. His name was Georges, and Salt had ordered him to guide three Japanese to the airfield and help them kill Mr. M. The three Japanese were near the car, talking low among themselves. Two spoke a little English, as did Georges.

Turning to face them, he whispered, "Listen. Car. Sounds like a car."

The three Japanese stepped forward quickly, their feet echoing on the concrete floor of the hangar. The leader, a powerfully built bearded man named Yuri, moved beside Georges, his slant eyes narrowing in suspicion. "Yes," he hissed. "Car."

His lips pressed tightly together, perspiration gleaming on his flat-nosed face despite the April chill, Charles Clary kept his foot on the accelerator, his mouth dry with fright, his head light with the excitement of what he would do in the next ten seconds.

The car bumped and jerked over holes, chunks of wood and pieces of misshapen concrete. Still without headlights, he covered the last fifteen feet between him and the plane.

The car jammed the tail of the small blue plane, the crash echoing across the quiet, dark countryside. Spinning around, the plane skipped and fluttered like a huge bird trying to get off the ground with one wing. Pieces of the car clanged to the concrete, and the front bumper dragged along the runway, sending orange sparks left and right.

Fighting hard, Clary fought for control of his car, now sliding sideways away from the damaged plane, turning in its own half-circle.

Gripping the wheel hard, Clary swung the car around, aiming it at the rear of the giant wounded plane bumping along in front of him. Gray smoke trailed from behind it like a giant piece of tissue. In the darkness of the hangar, two headlights flashed on brightly and a car's motor roared to life, unheard over the duel between plane and car.

The bearded Japanese, Yuri, had turned, barked an order, and the man nearest the car jumped in, turning on the motor and the headlights. As Georges, Yuri, and the third Japanese moved quickly toward the car, the black Samurai stepped from the darkness into the front of the hangar, pointed his .45 at the car, and fired three times.

The powerful triple roar of the gun filled the hangar, echoing again and again, drowning out the sound of broken glass falling to the concrete floor. Sand had shot out the headlights and the left front tire. Quickly, he stepped inside the hangar and to the left, crouching. Voices spoke quickly in Japanese, and he heard footsteps as the killers ducked behind the car.

He had picked his cover in the few seconds he stood in the front of the hangar. Rusted oil drums to his left. The rust told him the drums were empty, and not about to explode from gunfire.

He heard a voice say in Japanese, "No flashlight, you fool. He's not blind, damn it!"

An important break. The black Samurai had used darkness before, he would use it again.

He heard them whispering in Japanese. He smiled to himself. They would never believe that someone in the French countryside spoke Japanese. And a black man at that.

The attackers were splitting up. Two around each end of the car, and at a signal from Yuri, they began creeping along the sides of the hangar in darkness, toward the front.

The black Samurai didn't have long to wait.

The killers moved quickly, making only small noises. Saraga's men were good. Even in darkness, in unfamiliar ground, they moved well. Sand, who had trained in dark rooms, his bare hands against a man wielding a 30-inch Samurai sword, had learned to use his ears to see. Tonight, he saw well.

He lowered his breathing, taking in air in short, shallow breaths. He froze in place, facing the direction at least two men would be coming at him from. Dressed in black leather, he crouched in darkness, waiting. Saraga's killers were good. Sand was better.

They were almost on him. Small sounds—breathing, a man shifting, coins in someone's pocket, the safety catch being taken off a gun. Sand heard the sounds and he used them.

The .45 was tucked in the small of his back. Now he used his fighting skills.

Instinct and reflexes told him where to strike.

In the darkness, the knife edge of his right hand swung in a flat, strong arc, crushing the throat of a man whose face he had never seen and could not see now. As the man fell backward in the darkness, Sand was on him, attacking instinctively. Two short quick punches from his right fist landed in the softness of the man's testicles.

Continuing to move with stunning speed, his right leg lashed out in a roundhouse kick, smashing into the base of the spine of the second man in the darkness. The man cried out, spinning around on tiptoe to ease the agony racing up his back.

His back now to the man, Sand drove his right elbow hard into the man's stomach, dropping his right fist lower and banging the side of it into the man's balls.

Quickly, Sand shouted in Japanese, "I have him, I have him!" Then he leaped behind the rusted oil drums, a fraction of a second before flashlights sliced through the darkness. The .45 was in his hand and he was breathing hard. Footsteps came toward him, then angled off to the side as Yuri and the Frenchman moved toward Sand's shout.

A second later he stood up, moving closer to the two men. "Stay!" he commanded. "Don't turn. Guns, flashlights on the floor. Just bend over easy. You can live if you're careful."

The tight-fitting black woolen ski mask muffled his voice.

Yuri and the Frenchman moved stiffly, bending over and doing as ordered. Before Sand could say a word, Charles Clary said behind him, "Robert, I—"

The black Samurai half turned his head toward the sound of Clary's voice, and Yuri struck. The powerful bearded Japanese turned his head quickly toward Sand. Then his right leg came up in a high back kick, timing and distance perfect, smashing the .45 from Sand's fingers, paining and numbing his hand and wrist.

Georges squatted quickly, his fingers fumbling in darkness for a gun on the dirty hangar floor.

Yelling "Kiaaai!" Sand moved forward toward Yuri and Georges, then left his feet in a high leap, stretching his right leg out as far as he could in a desperate powerful thrust kick aimed at Georges. If the Frenchman got a gun, it was all over for the black Samurai.

Sand took a dangerous risk. In attacking Georges, he left himself exposed to Yuri. But there was no other choice. The black Samurai's right foot smashed into the base of Georges's skull, sending him falling forward, long, damp hair flying wildly about his head. When Georges's face met the concrete, he never felt it.

A fraction of a second later, however, the black Samurai felt pain. As Sand landed on the concrete hangar floor, knees bent to cushion the shock, Yuri drove a swift roundhouse kick to his head. Instinctively, Sand's left arm came up to block it, but he had to take pain to stop the attack. Yuri's attacks were strong, and unlike the other men Sand had fought tonight, he was ready. And good. Damn good.

The power of his attack drove Sand down hard to his knees on the concrete floor. Yelling, Yuri stepped in, driving the edge of his stiffened hand straight down toward Sand's neck and collarbone. It would be a blow strong enough to kill or break bone.

Still on his knees, Sand crossed both of his own hands at the wrists, then drove them up high and caught Yuri's wrist. Without hesitating, Yuri powered his knee at Sand's head. Sand leaned his head to the right, but the knee grazed his left temple and the red pain raced crazily around his skull.

Falling completely on his right side, Sand lashed out hard with his left leg, smashing Yuri in the left knee. The bearded Japanese killer backed off, stumbling, hurt but still dangerous.

Rolling to his feet, his head dizzy with the knee attack, Sand opened his eyes wider, quickly trying to focus on the powerfully built, bearded killer. He saw him move back a short step, favoring the left knee.

Sand moved swiftly. Stepping forward, he faked a quick left punch at Yuri's head, then stepping quickly to the right, he forced the Japanese to attempt to shift on a left leg that was not as strong as it had been seconds earlier.

Pain and blackness reached out for the masked black Samurai, but he willed himself to fight. Yelling at the top of his lungs, he unleashed a powerful kick at Yuri's stomach with his left leg, then kicked with his right leg, again forcing Yuri to defend.

The bearded Japanese blocked each attack, his power blocks sending pain up Sand's legs. But the black Samurai had learned what he needed to know. The kick in the knee had hurt Yuri, because now he just blocked, and did not attack.

Sand finished him off.

Swiftly he moved in, throwing a strong kick at Yuri's right knee. As Yuri moved the right leg back from harm, his face grim and determined to fight until death, his left leg was forward and exposed. Still moving forward, Sand swept the ankle, catching it with his own right leg.

He saw Yuri's eyes glaze with pain and defeat, as he went down hard on the filthy concrete. Sand was on him, twice driving powerful blows into his temple.

Yuri rolled over on his right side, then flopped onto his back, his arms spread wide.

Sand's chest heaved and he breathed loudly. Tearing the ski mask from his face, he looked at Clary standing in the beam of a flashlight that was still on the floor.

In a voice almost too soft to be heard, Clary said, "I've seen fighters, but none like you. Absolutely no one fights as well as you."

"The pilot?" said Sand, pressing his lips together to squeeze the pain out of his head.

"Alive, sort of."

Turning, Sand picked up his .45, his fingers numb, the bones of his forearms throbbing with pain. Then walking toward Clary, he moved past him out of the hangar and toward the smoking plane now leaning to one side, a wing touching the runway.

"Let's see what 'sort of' means."

CHAPTER 7

Final Payment

Valbonne was angry. He chewed a corner of his lip, his eyes blazing, as he listened to Pierre Roth.

"It cannot be helped, Mr. Valbonne. The German is old, too old for this kind of hard work, and we are pushing him along with the rest. He's 70 years old, Mr. Valbonne, and cold mountain weather like this in Switzerland is too much for him. He's used to Egypt, where it's a lot warmer and—"

Valbonne's voice snapped like a whip beating against a brick wall. "Roth, I don't give a damn if he dies, so long as he dies *after* he finishes that bomb! We've got three German scientists and seven technicians. This old man coughing blood is the one who best knows *exactly* what has to be done."

"Mr. Valbonne, I—"

"Shut up! Peter Holz is worth millions of dollars to me and he's not going to die! Understand that, Roth. Holz *will* live!"

Roth, nervously fingering the dark glasses he wore day or night, tried to hold Valbonne's strong green-eyed stare, but as always, he turned away, his lips pressed tightly together, his stomach churning as though filled with broken glass. Valbonne had that effect on people.

It wasn't Roth's fault that the old German was coming apart like wet newspaper. Third time he had gotten sick. Damn! Valbonne was driving all of them like slaves, working them around the clock, making all of the scientific people sleep, eat, work in the same building. At least Roth and Valbonne's other men were allowed to go into Geneva and see women once in a while.

Those working directly on the bomb weren't that lucky. Even though they were paid well, cash directly or in deposits in numbered Swiss bank accounts, whichever they preferred. Those young enough for sex, or interested in it, were serviced by prostitutes hired by Valbonne once every ten days.

Sex took place at Valbonne's chateau, with a minimum of conversation. But the bomb was being built fifteen miles away, in a small snow-covered valley. The valley had two hills in front and to the side a small grove of trees. Valbonne hadn't picked it for the view. He had picked it because of an abandoned ski lodge, and a crude but usable road, and a small abandoned weather station on top of one hill.

Permits and papers had been obtained showing that Valbonne was reopening the ski lodge, carefully rebuilding it. That had been four months ago. Should anyone ask about it or come looking in the small, deserted valley, Valbonne had an explanation for men, trucks and activity occasionally seen in that area.

The weather station on one hill served as a lookout post. Another small shack had been hastily built on the other hill. Both were manned by armed guards 24 hours a day. Supplies and materials were almost always trucked in at night. By day, huge signs in three languages reading "Private Property—Keep Off" or "Danger—Construction" were enough to keep strangers from the area.

Still, the armed guards kept huge black binoculars to their eyes and powerful scoped rifles near fingers numbed with cold.

Four months ago.

Now trouble.

At the moment, Valbonne didn't care whose fault it was. He was enraged. "So close," he yelled. "So damn close and this old bastard has to start coughing blood. Days away from success and more money than any man's made in this business. I wish I didn't need him. I'd like to throw him naked in the snow and let him cough until he chokes. He escapes the Russians and the Americans, spends fifteen years hiding in South America, and even manages to escape the Jews, who have been damn good at catching up with Nazis. Five years in Spain, nine years in Egypt, and nows he gets sick. Now!"

Roth cringed, his eyes blinking behind the dark glasses.

He knew why Valbonne was almost foaming at the mouth. Peter Holz was old, sure, and his thin hands, brown-spotted with age, trembled like a feather in an earthquake. But the old German bastard was smart.

Even Roth knew that. He knew enough German to understand the three German scientists' excitement when they found out that the atomic bomb they were building for Valbonne and Saraga would weigh only 2,000 pounds. It could easily be broken down into four parts and carried on trucks to Saraga's ships. The bomb dropped on Nagasaki in 1945 had weighed 10,000 pounds.

Yeah, he understood why Valbonne needed the old man.

"Mr. Valbonne, I'll bring the car around. We'll drive him down to the chateau and have the doctor come out from Geneva just like before. He can treat him there and the old man will be back at work maybe even today, if the doctor's in."

Valbonne's nostrils flared and his loud breathing was the only sound in the empty front room of the phony ski lodge. "Do that, Roth!" he snapped. "Do that!" For a few seconds, his green eyes burned into the Frenchman as though attempting to smash his dark glasses with the intensity of his stare. Then—"I'm going downstairs to talk with the others to see if we can avoid any delay. One thing, Roth. Stay with Holz while the doctor's treating him. Don't let him out of your sight, understand?"

Roth licked his lips in nervousness. He understood. He'd make the call from the chateau. There was no phone in the ski lodge. All communication between Valbonne's home and the lodge was by radio. He and two guards would have to drive the old German out of the snow-covered valley, along the bumpy road, then down to Valbonne's chateau where there was less snow and better roads.

Anything to get away from Valbonne. If Roth wasn't making fantastic money, he'd find a way to push Valbonne into some of that radioactive material stored behind lead doors in the basement. That would fix the little bastard's ass, providing that crazy Apache Indian, Salt, didn't see Roth do the pushing. Then it would be *Roth's* ass.

But what the hell, Valbonne had promised Roth a $100,000 bonus when the bomb was delivered, and for that kind of money, Roth would take a lot of Valbonne's shit.

Dr. Otto Perrin wiped the pale-blue vein with a small piece of alcohol-soaked cotton, then quickly and smoothly slid the needle into the vein, easing his thumb off the needle's plunger. His keen blue eyes watched until all of the yellow liquid eased from the hypodermic into the sleeping old man.

Removing the needle, he dabbed the invisible hole with the cotton and, without turning to look at Pierre Roth, said in French, "This will let him rest for an hour or two at least. He should have more. He's rundown, exhausted, quite tired. I don't know what he's been doing, but he's doing too much of it. Rest, good food are necessary. I'm going to give him a vitamin shot, but I want him to start taking vitamins on his own. I'll leave you the list."

Roth's fingers nervously touched his dark glasses, pushing them back onto his nose. He coughed to clear his throat, then said, "Thank you, doctor, but is there any way we, I mean, can he be ready to, well . . ."

Snapping his lean head around, blond hair sliding down his forehead, Perrin said briskly, "This man needs rest. If he doesn't get it he will die. If you care about him, you'll see that this does not happen."

Roth nodded, saying nothing.

Standing up, the doctor walked to a table, sat down, and began to write prescriptions and a list of vitamins. "Take care of these immediately. Call me if he begins to develop a fever. Don't wait. He's not a young man, remember that."

Roth wasn't about to forget it. Valbonne wasn't about to let him.

Ten minutes later, Dr. Perrin was in his snow-covered blue Volkswagen, his heart pounding, his eyes staring at the road, trying hard to concentrate. When he reached Geneva, he was going to do two things.

The first thing was to have a tall glass of straight scotch.

The second thing was to contact William Baron Clarke.

"I figured now's as a good a time as any," said the Baron. He sat on the edge of the wide bed, combing his silver-colored hair with his fingers. "French sumbitches think I'm gonna die soon, so they're anxious to photograph me for some kind of historical museum their government's got goin'. Say, son, pass me that eye opener, will ya?"

He pointed to a half-bottle of bourbon on the dresser. Robert Sand picked up the bottle and looked around for a clean glass.

"Skip the glass." The Baron held his hand out for the bottle, then put it to his lips, leaning his head back. Sand watched his adam's apple bobbing again and again. "Ahhh," said the tall Texan. "Now this is the way to see Paris. Goddam town would be all right if it wasn't for all the Frenchmen in it."

Sand smiled. It was ten o'clock in the morning. Clarke was in Paris to be photographed for posterity and to attend a reception in his honor by the French government. His hotel room overlooked the Champs Élysées.

"Wife's out shoppin'. No trouble gettin' her to do that in this town. She'll call before she comes back. Women will spend money as long as somebody's printin' it. Love that gal."

The Baron also loved secrecy. Sand's caution had always impressed him, and except on rare occasions, their meetings involved only each other. "Food's got to be better here than in Korea," said Clarke. "Whatever I ate there two days ago, I don't think was dead when they put it on the plate."

"Valbonne," said Sand.

The Baron made a face, then took another pull from the bourbon, wiping his mouth with the back of his hand. "Three names. First is Otto Perrin, a doctor in Geneva. He confirms that one of the German atomic scientists working for Valbonne is Peter Holz. I sent him a small picture I got from Egypt. It's Holz, all right, and he's in Switzerland like you said. Perrin can only go there when he's asked out, but he's treated Holz three times so far. Says the old German's in a bad way, might not live out the next month. Probably got Valbonne worried crazy. Confirms your information. Bomb has to be in Switzerland someplace."

"Egypt," said Sand. "What did you get there?"

"Confirmed what you got from Turpin. Holz and another German scientist named Mueller left there five months ago. My contact thinks money helped, because the Germans had to bribe somebody to get out of Cairo. Egyptians don't have the money or facilities or even the inclination to make an A-bomb. They talk a good game, but my feelin' is they're waitin' on the Russians to sell

them somethin'. Might just happen one day. Guess Mueller and Holz got tired of doing nothin'.' "

"You said you had three names?"

"Yep. Second is Ford. Otis Ford. Black, American and
captain of the *Excalibur*." Excalibur. The name of King
Arthur's sword.

Excalibur. Valbonne's display case, a floating gun shop.
A cargo ship with guns, tanks, bombs, radios—samples
of the armaments Valbonne was offering for sale. It sailed
all over the world, showing the samples, taking orders.

"Ford," said the Baron, "is pissed. Ain't makin' the
money he feels he should. Worse, he's scared out of his
black skin at even the thought of that Apache. He and
Salt don't get along in spades, 'scuse me son. Wants his
own ship, feels he can get it faster by passing on information to me. I encourage such thoughts and give him
60,000 tax-free dollars a year besides. Might be tough for
him to 'get out' 'cause he knows a lot about Valbonne's
business."

"Third name?"

"Female. Pretty. Very special lady. Name's Zoraida
Mahon, she's Spanish-Irish, 26, smart as hell, and she
works for Saraga. Right now he's got her acting as his
courier. She's makin' payments to Valbonne, the advance
on the bomb."

"How do you know this?"

The Baron grinned, his tanned face creasing. Rolling
the almost empty bourbon bottle between his large, gnarled
hands, he chuckled and said slyly, " 'Cause I'm goddam
smart, that's why. Saraga's got a lot of people handlin'
his money. One of 'em thinks Saraga's crazier than a man
kicked in the head twelve times by a horse. Man's name
is Ganai and he's a Tokyo banker. Now ol' Mr. Ganai heard
that a certain American oil company's gonna try to look
for oil offshore around Japan. You any idea how
hungry that country is for oil?"

"Like a drowning man wants air," said Sand.

"Rightee. Mr. Ganai wants in on that company as maybe its Japanese head. I own 25 percent of that company.
And that, my black friend, is how I come to own 100
percent of Mr. Ganai. He's been damn good at lettin' me
know about Saraga's money. That's how I know Saraga's
been shiftin' yen, dollars, francs, marks to come up with
the advance payment. Almost $50 million, somethin' like

maybe $10 million a month for the past five months, has been partly deposited in Swiss banks for Valbonne and in part hand-carried to Switzerland by our Miss Zoraida Mahon. Mr. Ganai wants to be a Japanese president of an American oil company awfully bad. So he's been good about keepin' me informed."

Sand nodded. He was impressed.

" 'Nother thing. Ganai and the girl don't know why all that money's goin' to Valbonne. They don't know about the bomb. Saraga's got them both thinkin' he's working a deal for gold, with Valbonne as the middleman."

Sand said, "That won't help either one of them. When the time comes, they'll be killed. They know just enough to qualify as knowing too much."

"Maybe. Can't say as how you're wrong, since you been runnin' into Valbonne's clean-up squad lately. Anyway, I can keep you posted on the gal's moves. How you get close to her is your business. You'll meet with Ford. He knows something but not too much about the bomb. He's sure it's not at Valbonne's chateau; he's been there many times. He doesn't really believe this whole thing will go through, but that's for you and me to deal with."

Sand nodded. "One thing's more or less sure. The bomb's in Switzerland somewhere. That's the reason for Turpin making phony Swiss passport and papers for Peter Holz. *Where* is the problem. And the trigger device—we need to know its whereabouts. One thing I've been meaning to ask you. Who first told you about this bomb?"

The Baron looked serious, his fingernails scratching his unshaven chin. "Man named Ian Berk. Ain't heard from him lately. Hope that don't mean the Apache's been practicin' on him."

Ian Berk. Sand knew the name. A British scientist who had defected to Red China two years ago, dropping out of sight.

The Baron stood up, stretching and yawning. "Berk had some kind of fallin' out with the Chinese communists, so one fine day he manages to get himself out of the country, with help from our Mr. Saraga. For months he just hangs around Saraga's house, doin' nothin'! That's when he and I made contact. Suddenly Saraga's got a chore for him. Berk's goin' back in the A-bomb business. He's gonna be the dude, Saraga says, who'll let him know just whether or not Valbonne's keepin' his promises or just jerkin' Saraga off. Our Mr. Berk was picked to watch the bomb and report to Saraga. He was less than happy about this little chore, but then Saraga laid it on him: do it or end up back in Peking with somebody slicing at your balls with a dull knife. So Berk got this last message out about the bomb and I ain't heard hide nor hair from him since."

"Any idea where he is now?"

"Last time I heard from him it was from Japan, but he may be right next to the bomb so as to let Saraga know he's gettin' his money's worth."

Sand nodded. "If I find him, I'll know just about all I need to know."

"Damn right. One more piece of news. Ol' Mr. Ganai's been told by Saraga to help him get $50 million ready about ten or twelve days from now. No later."

Sand snapped his face toward the Baron. The black Samurai narrowed his eyes and looked as though the room was on fire. "He's told you more than you know."

"What do you mean?"

"That's the final payment. The bomb will be ready for delivery then. It means they plan to trigger if off in New York in about two weeks or less."

The Baron stared at Sand. "How you figger? How come that ain't just another in the series of payments?"

"Because it's too large, because it matches the total money the woman and the banker have already delivered. Don't you see, it's the final payment. It's payment on delivery."

Clarke's face was grim and unsmiling. "Sometimes, son, you're just too goddam smart. And too goddam right. We got us a row to hoe, and no time to do it. Let's get crackin'. Soon as my hands stop shakin', I plan to shave. Meanwhile, tell me about that pilot you got stashed away, and do an old man a favor. Call downstairs and have them send up two more bottles of mother's milk. I'm gonna need it."

Mother's milk. The Baron's name for bourbon.

CHAPTER 8

Berk

Salt said, "Two of Saraga's men are dead, and two more are hurtin' bad. I figure it's the same dude in both cases, the nigger. Forget that ski-mask shit at the hangar. If it was a different guy, he'd make sure we knew it. Hidin' like that just means one man."

The Apache spoke slowly, carefully, into the telephone, his voice even, sure of his words and thoughts.

Valbonne listened attentively. The Apache was no intellectual, but he was shrewd in matters of killing and men who killed. He was probably right about what had happened. But who was the black man? Why was he making these attacks on Valbonne's men?

"Mangas, this new problem comes at a bad time. I am having difficulty with one of the Germans. His health. You know the man I'm speaking of. I just want to ask you, do you feel we have someone passing on information to outsiders?"

"Anything's possible, Mr. Valbonne. Like I always told you, I ain't never liked that nigger Ford you got running your ship. I know that it's your business who you hire and everything, but I just don't dig the guy, that's all."

"Mangas, are you saying Otis Ford is an informant for somebody? He is an excellent sailor, and knows his job well. Despite his trouble in the American Navy, I've always found him quite competent." Valbonne was shrewd enough to know that the Indian resented an educated black man, especially one with Ford's position. Jealousy and racial prejudice. But the Frenchman needed the Apache, and Ford was a good ship captain.

But if Ford were an informant, well—

65

"Mangas, I must go now. Urgent business. What do you suggest?"

A corner of the Apache's lips moved upward, but his hard brown eyes did not match the tiny smile of his cruel mouth. "A trap, Mr. Valbonne. Let me handle it my way. If Ford's straight, no sweat. But if he's setting us up, he's mine."

"Yes, Mangas. Your way seems reasonable to me. Keep in touch. How long will it take you to, say, arrange things?"

"Not long, Mr. Valbonne. I still have other names on that list. Say less than two days for Mr. Ford. At the end of that time, we'll know which direction he's facin', ours or somebody else's."

"Keep in touch, Mangas." Click. The phone went dead. The huge Apache leaned his head back, his eyes narrowing. Ford.

Salt smiled. The smile was cruel and frightening.

Ian Berk was paying for a mistake.

His beating by two of Valbonne's men was quick, brutal, efficient. A lesson in manners. The bearded British scientist had been told to do something and had refused.

In the small, cold and gray concrete room in the basement of the ski lodge, Valbonne leaned against a wall and watched with casual interest. "His face," he said. "Don't touch it."

Grunting in reply, his back to Valbonne, a bald-headed German wrestler drove a huge fist into the tall, thin scientist's back, sending agony flashing from Berk's kidneys and across every inch of skin on his body. Berk squealed, a high-pitched sound like an animal on fire. The sound would not go past the concrete walls.

Valbonne's voice snapped. "On the floor, face down."

Berk knelt on his knees facing the wall, his fingernails digging into the concrete on either side of him, his face pressed sideways against the cool surface. He breathed through his mouth, slowly and loud, the hoarse sound easing into a moan.

The two muscular Germans pulled him away from the wall and dropped him face down on the damp concrete floor. "His little finger," said Valbonne. "He's right-handed, so make it his left hand."

Without a word, one of the Germans jammed a huge booted foot down on Berk's left hand, mashing it into the concrete. Then, reaching over, the German gripped the British scientist's little finger and with a swift motion, pulled it backward until it snapped.

Berk cried out, lifting his head from the concrete. "Oh God, Jesus God." A long loud moan came from him. Timeless, wordless agony. He passed out, his head flopping back to the concrete.

"Wake him," said Valbonne, rubbing his own hands together for warmth.

The Germans turned Berk over on his back. Then one of them crouched over the unconscious scientist and slapped his face twice. Berk moaned, his head moving side to side.

Valbonne walked over and, smiling, looked down at Berk. "My way, Mr. Berk. My way and no other. You do not say no to me. Not ever. I will tell you what to do and you will do it. Next time, the beating will last longer, and I will have *two* more of your fingers broken. Your face is unmarked, which makes it unnecessary for you to indulge in prolonged explanations to your co-workers. As for your finger, I will give you an excuse for that."

Painfully, Berk rolled to his side and raised himself to one hip. His mouth hung open and he gulped air greedily. Slowly he rolled to a sitting position, his left hand cupped in his right.

"You will work on the bomb, Mr. Berk. Your expertise is needed because Peter Holz's health is poor at the moment. There is too much at stake here for me to allow you the luxury of being just an observer and houseguest. If you think Mr. Saraga will defend your point of view, you are a fool, sir, a classic fool. He wants revenge and your life is a small price to pay for it. When you refused me, when you said you would not work on our project, well, I can only say, Mr. Berk, that fools like you are expendable. Your hand will be bandaged, and I expect you in the laboratory in fifteen minutes."

Berk sat on the cold concrete floor, rubbing his left hand. Tears glistened brightly on his bearded face, and his chin trembled as he fought to keep from weeping out loud. His broken finger was an ugly purple. He was in pain and badly frightened.

Valbonne shuddered with the chill, his green eyes still burning into the beaten man sitting on the floor. "You speak German fluently, Mr. Berk, so there should be no

trouble with Holz's notes. Some of the other personnel speak English and can fill you in. You will remain in
the laboratory until I come for you, and you will do your
best. If I hear differently from your co-workers, I shall
give your body over to my Apache friend while you are
still among the living. Believe me when I tell you, your
death will be a classic in suffering. So work well, Mr.
Berk. You will be rewarded and you will also be alive,
which may well be the best reward of all."

Valbonne's green eyes snapped to the two huge Germans
and he signaled them to move in on Berk. "See that he
is in good working order, gentlemen."

Valbonne's footsteps pounded across the concrete floor,
and he was gone, the door slamming shut behind him.

Tenderly, the two Germans lifted Berk off the floor,
holding him gently as though he were a dear friend, as
though they had come upon him in his agony just seconds
ago.

They were pros. Beating him had been just a part of
the job. Caring for him was another part, and they would
do both parts well.

Blood trickled from a corner of Berk's mouth, and one
of the Germans wiped it away with his fingertips, as
though Berk were a young boy who had tripped in the
schoolyard. In a gentle voice, the German said, "Ah, my
friend, you will have trouble pissing for a while, I'm
afraid. Your kidneys. Sorry, friend."

Berk didn't hear him. He was unconscious, his bearded,
sweating chin hanging down in defeat, his mind gripped
by the hideous dream of his fingers breaking painfully.
The horrible snapping sound of breaking bone suddenly
caused him to open his bloodshot eyes wide and scream
aloud.

Talking eased Otis Ford's mind away from the cold fear
wrapped tightly around him. He said to Robert Sand, "Yeah,
brother, I know Ian Berk. Looks thinner now than he does
in that snapshot you got. Working for Valbonne can kill
your appetite. Baby, I ought to know."

The two black men sat in the front seat of Ford's
custom $40,000 Mercedes, parked on a quiet road outside
of Paris. Above them the sky was streaked orange and red
by the setting sun. It would be dark in less than an hour.

Sand carefully eyed the lean, light-brown-skinned captain of Valbonne's gun ship, the *Excalibur*. Otis Ford's fingers, in $80 tan cashmere gloves, nervously drummed the red-leather-wrapped steering wheel. His Black Diamond mink coat, worn against the April Paris chill, caught bright patches of fading sunlight. The lumps under the back of Ford's gloves were caused by three diamond rings.

"Word's around that Racine's dead," said Ford. "Vain's gettin' wasted ain't no secret either. Everybody knows, baby, everybody. What goes around comes around. But tying it up with Valbonne, well . . ." His voice trailed off.

"You're fooling yourself," said Sand, his keen eyes on Ford's face. "You know Valbonne did it. He's capable of killing or having it done. You also know I'm right about Saraga wanting an atomic bomb to use on New York City. Your eyes say so, your face says so. You know the truth, Ford. It's time to take your hands away from your eyes, because whatever darkness you're in at the moment won't last long."

Ford let out a deep breath, reaching inside his mink coat and pulling out a flat silver case. Plucking out a thin gold-tipped black cigar and slipping it between his lips, he offered Robert Sand one. Sand shook his head side to side in refusal.

Ford flicked open the jaws of a thin gold lighter, touched flame to the slender cigar, inhaling deeply. The lighter closed with a sharp click. "I'm 33 and I want out. But baby, it ain't easy. I know too much about Valbonne's guns. And ain't nothing that fucking crazy Apache would like more than to peel the skin off my black ass with a razor blade. He's crazy enough to do it, know what I'm saying? There's a hole in my stomach, an ulcer, and those two dudes put it there. I tried pluggin' up that hole with money, brother, but it don't go down that way."

Sand said nothing. Money. That's what had cost Otis Ford a career in the United States Navy. While serving in Vietnam, he had gone into the black market and gotten caught. Getting caught was followed by a court-martial and getting kicked out. After that, the rest was easy, too easy. Valbonne offered a command, the *Excalibur*, and fistfuls of money.

Today, Ford was admitting to himself and Sand that he had said yes to more things than he had realized. "The Baron. Is he really straight? Can he help me?"

"Yes. A lot more than you can help Berk."

Berk. That's why the two men were sitting in the parked car in fading sunlight. Four miles away was a small zoo. Ian Berk was supposed to be there, waiting for Ford to come and pick him up, take him onboard ship, then drop him in Italy. From there, Berk would get a boat to Africa and hide from Valbonne and anyone else looking for him. That's what the note had said. The note had been waiting for Ford at his Paris hotel.

Ford had three days away from the ship, now docked in Calais, while oil-rich and gun-hungry Arabs looked over Valbonne's supply of weapons. The note also said that Berk would pay Ford $50,000, and money was something the black sea captain always needed desperately. If Berk was willing to buy his freedom, Ford was even more willing to insure his own.

Sand read the note, passing it back to Ford without a comment. But the black Samurai's eyes narrowed for a few seconds as his mind picked at him. One thing bothered him. With Peter Holz seriously ill, Berk was worth his weight in platinum to Valbonne. Meaning Berk wouldn't be alone any hour of the day or night, let alone get the chance to escape.

Sand kept his thoughts to himself.

"Salt's killed people before," said Ford. "I guess I closed my eyes to that, too. He hates me because I'm black, smarter than he is, and maybe even because I can read without moving my lips, something I ain't too sure that sucker can do. Reason he ain't done shit to me so far is Valbonne. Got me a piece, a Beretta, small thing, pussy pistol you might call it. Don't know if it can stop him, sure hope I don't have to find out."

"When did you see Berk last?"

"Hmmm, 'bout a month ago. Did some partying together. Valbonne had some whores in from Geneva, English, Swedish, German broads. Berk, me, 'bout four other guys who I've seen at the chateau from time to time. Man, we all hit on them bitches, took ourselves one, then paired off in a room somewhere. Hey, know what Valbonne said, don't know if he was kiddin' or not. Says one day he's gonna play me some tapes of me fuckin'. Guess that means he's got tape recorders in the rooms." Ford smiled weakly, a gloved finger touching his black mustache.

"Did Berk give his name?"

"Just his first name, Ian. Didn't say much except that he was working on something with Valbonne and would be around Geneva for a while. Fact is, none of the other guys talked about themselves, either. But with the broads and shit, well, you know. I mean, like, who the hell cared."

"Any of the men speak German?"

"Hmmm, yeah, yeah. Two did. Say, you really think Berk's got $50,000?"

Sand nodded. "Saraga's giving Valbonne $100 million. I'm betting Valbonne's bomb builders do the job for less than that. It's been 29 years since the atomic bomb dropped on people, but you can bet there are men smart enough to come up with an improved bomb in no time at all. Especially for money."

Ford blew small, rounded smoke rings. He put one gloved hand in his pocket to keep it from shaking.

Sand thought to himself how important Berk must be to Valbonne at the moment. Berk. The key man, the man who would know about the bomb, the target date, how it's coming into America. Berk.

Aloud he said, "Any airfield near the chateau?"

"No. We talked about building one, but the ground's too hard most of the year. Frozen. Land isn't level around there. Don't know why Valbonne's so hot about building a ski lodge near there."

Sand's brown eyes grew bright with interest. "Ski lodge?"

"Yeah. Sometimes he forgets this nigger speaks French. Came to the chateau one day, hear him on the phone yelling to somebody that they had damn well better get him the building permit and other papers he needed for the ski lodge. Man, he was yelling something fierce 'bout those papers. Guess that explains those trucks that been coming by the chateau by night."

Ski lodge. Trucks. And all information on Valbonne saying he rarely leaves his chateau. Berk in Switzerland at least until a month ago. Berk who knew all about Saraga's atomic bomb.

"Valbonne say anything about your taking off today?"

"No way. I'm a damn good captain, even if I do work for Valbonne. I'll be back when I should be. No, he didn't mind at all."

Sand said, "Stay here. Have to make a phone call."

In less than a minute, he was inside the café across the road and speaking with the Baron. Later, outside, he stood on the sidewalk as a truck went by, then he crossed the road and slipped back inside the Mercedes. "Let's go to the zoo," he said.

He didn't tell Ford the Baron was surprised as hell to hear about Ian Berk's getting away from Valbonne. The Baron wondered why the hell he hadn't heard from Berk.

The black Samurai wondered about that, too.

CHAPTER 9

Ambush

The stench from the animals' cages reached out for him, making Otis Ford cringe. His tense brown face twisted in revulsion and he coughed twice. He was alone in the small ape house. Just him and the quiet animals—apes, monkeys. And two empty cages.

Heart pounding, he stepped forward softly, waving a cashmere-gloved hand in front of his nose in a vain attempt to brush away the stink as well as the stale smell of damp straw caked with animal shit.

Dried, blackened fruit lay on the gray concrete floors of cages like abandoned children's toys. Ford licked his lips in nervousness, then ground his teeth together in tension. Where the fuck was that British bastard? It was his idea to meet in this funky-ass place. Damn! This odor was enough to melt your balls.

He walked forward into the almost darkened building, stepping softly on bright-orange ribbons of fading sunlight coming through the opened door behind him. Berk, you prick, where the hell are you. You'd better be here, Jack, with the $50,000, too.

Shit. First soulbrother Robert makes me stop the car a half-mile away, then he gets out, tells me to wait ten minutes before coming to the zoo, he takes his black ass off on foot and disappears. Doesn't say shit 'bout where he's goin' or why, just splits, man. Strange dude, old Robert. No last name, just Robert. But he looks like he ain't nobody to jive with.

Ford lifted his left wrist up, pushing the Black Diamond mink back along his arm, twisting his wrist to catch the sunlight. Five-fifteen. Berk was fifteen minutes late, and it was getting darker outside than an eclipse in Harlem. Shit! OK, that's cool. When that dude did show up, Ford was going to kick his ass if he didn't have the bread.

The sounds came from behind him, and his heart jumped. He turned, mouth dry with tension and fear. "Berk—?"

Black shapes filled the door, silhouetted against the fading, deep orange of the sun. He saw no faces. Just menacing black shapes moving slowly toward him. In panic, he tore open his mink coat, his gloved hand tearing at his waistband. As his fingers touched the Beretta, a voice came from the black shapes closing in on him.

"Nigger, you touch that pussy pistol and you ain't got no more time left on God's earth."

Ford's hand froze in place.

Salt. His flat, slow way of talking. His voice coming out of the darkness, the sum of all the terrors Ford had ever feared in his entire lifetime.

Salt.

The black shapes stopped, three of them spreading right and left, forming a half-circle.

"Put the Beretta on the ground, then kick it over here easy-like."

Ford, his eyes toward the sound of the Apache's voice, bent down slowly, lips pressed together, his legs weak with fear. Placing the gun down gently, he stood up, his eyes still toward Salt's voice. When Ford's right foot found the gun, he pushed it toward Salt.

The Apache's voice was cold, filled with a desire to cause pain. The thought flashed across Ford's mind that hearing Salt speak was like having icicles shoved up your ass. "Nigger's smart. That's nice, real nice. Now, let's talk about your friends."

Ford fought for control of himself. With an effort, he forced his fingers into fists so they wouldn't shake, and he wetted his mouth with spit. Now. "Look, Salt, what the fuck's going down, man? I—"

Salt laughed once, a hard sound. His flat-featured, cruel face slid out of the darkness to within feet of the black man. "Nigger, you are a fucking positive thinker, that's what you are. You gonna tell me why you're here, right? Well, I *know* why you're here."

The note from Ian Berk. It burned the coat pocket of Ford's Black Diamond mink like hot ice. Suddenly, the truth exploded inside him. Berk hadn't written that note!

Salt said, "You came by yourself, but I tell you something, snowball. That don't mean shit to me. 'Cause I got a feeling about you and it's a bad one. That's the Apache way, and it ain't ever been wrong. What we all gonna do is explore your goddam mind."

Ford shook his head side to side in small, tight gestures. "Valbonne's gonna have your balls for this, man." Then, he screamed, "No two ways about it, Chief Bullshit. Valbonne ain't gonna like you leanin' on me."

Salt's evil smile was made more hideous by the darkness and fading sunlight. "Tell you something, black boy. First, I ain't gonna lay a hand on you. Neither is anybody else here. Second, if you tell me what I think you're gonna tell me, Valbonne is gonna be happy to dance on your grave."

Ford stood rigid with fear. In Vietnam, he'd heard stories of torture by the Cong and by the GIs, too. He'd heard Arab terrorists come on board the *Excalibur* and get drunk, then brag about what they had done to Jews, tortures that began with knife and fire and ended with the Jew begging to be killed. Anyone could be broken. Anyone.

"You can scream your tail off, man," said Salt, "but it ain't gonna help your case worth a rat's ass. I got men outside, and this place is officially closed today. Ain't that cute, nigger? Closed."

Silence.

Then Salt's slow voice, each word edged in steel. "Over there, that empty cage. Climb in. And just give me a reason to force you. This way, you got a few seconds of life for sure. Get tough, you got shit."

Ford turned and walked slowly toward the empty cage. He ducked under a tarnished brass rail, then pulled the unlocked door open and climbed inside. His feet brushed against a rubber ball, sending it rolling silently across the cold straw-covered floor.

As he stepped to the side, both hands gripping the bars, a flashlight beam blinded him, and he put his hands up to block the light. A cage lock snapping shut made him stiffen as though the sound had been a gunshot. Behind him, he felt cold air coming from where a sliding door had been pulled up, leaving an open space leading to an outdoor cage.

"Fuckin' fur coat makes you look like an animal, you know that?"

Ford didn't answer. The flashlight beam danced over the entire empty cage, its harsh white light turning the smelly, gray cage even uglier than it was.

Ford's eyes flicked right and left. In the darkness, he saw the three men with Salt take newspapers from their pockets and roll them up. Then each man took a lighter from his pocket and thumbed it into flame, the small, flickering orange flames showing their hard faces. Two men were European whites, the third was Japanese.

Each stood still, rolled newspaper in his left hand, the small, flaming lighter in his right. They waited. Small sounds came through the open slot behind Ford, but his eyes and mind were glued in terror to the strange scene in front of him. The men with rolled newspapers and flaming lighters. And the huge Apache Indian, dressed in street clothes, holding a flashlight.

"Nigger, you are gonna do *some* talkin'," said Salt, and he stepped toward the cage.

The black Samurai moved toward the first man. Japanese, stocky, lying flat on his stomach, a Czech 7.62mm Model 52 semi-automatic rifle cradled in his arms. He was behind a tree on a small hill overlooking the rear of the ape house where Berk was meeting Ford. The rifleman had made it easy. He was smoking.

Robert Sand crept through the oncoming darkness toward the thin twisting ribbons of gray smoke floating and fading in front of him. His keen sense of smell had picked up the odor long before his eyes pinpointed the man. In the eight minutes before Ford had driven up, Sand had made a cautious circle around the small zoo. In that short time, he had learned a lot.

The ambush was to be a deadly one. But it had been set up quickly, which meant it was not a careful one. Two men in front, two in back of the ape house, each with a rifle and handgun.

The two out in back were Japanese, Saraga's men on loan to Valbonne. They had natural cover—trees, bushes, a small hill, and darkness. The two in front were Europeans, one slouched down in a car parked diagonally across from the ape house, the other in the darkened doorway of the snake house located directly in front of the ape house.

The black Samurai smiled at the impatience and restlessness of the man hiding in the car. Twice, the gunman had slowly rolled down a window for air, rolling it up again when he got too cold. Sand would have set the ambush differently, with the patient Japanese out front, the most conspicuous spot, and the restless Europeans in back.

Even with a hasty ambush, the Apache himself had moved cautiously. Sand recognized him because of his huge size. In half-darkness on the small hill, Sand had checked his watch. Ford was on time, but the Apache waited fifteen full minutes before moving from the shadows of the snake house and across the small space between him and the ape house. Four men were with him. Three went inside, one off to the left of the small squat, red-brick building.

Two men out front and one to the side. Salt inside with three.

The black Samurai nodded. They were prepared for war. From the number of men, it was obvious Salt expected more than just Otis Ford to show. Sand's training allowed him no room for weakness. He knew they were waiting for him.

He went to meet them. His way.

Sacho, the Japanese gunman, heard the small sound and snapped his head to the left, his fingers dropping the cigarette, both hands clawing at the Czech rifle.

Sand's elbow rammed into his temple, sending painful flashes of white and red across his brain. Sacho fell on his back, his arms spreading wide. Quickly, Sand straddled his chest, lifting his stiff hand high, then bringing it down hard in a deadly knife blow to the neck.

Moving quickly from the body of the unconscious Japanese, Sand picked up the rifle and shoved it barrel down into the cool, damp earth. He twisted it right, then left. Dropping the rifle, he bent over and pulled a VP70 German pistol from the Japanese's waistband. He removed the magazine, placed it in his belt, then ejected the one shell in the chamber.

He slipped away in the deep twilight, never once looking behind him.

Ito's hand dug into the back of his own neck, rubbing hard against the stiffness gripping his muscles. He hated France. Too cold, and the French food was too spicy. Raw fish, seaweed, rice. That was good enough for him. But he worked for Saraga and loyalty was everything in this kind of a situation. Loyalty to the warlord. That was the old days in Japan, but things hadn't changed that much. You still ended up killing whoever you were ordered to and you got to eat because of it. Old days, new days. Same thing.

Suddenly Ito froze, his fingers moving to the trigger of his Type 99 Japanese rifle. Then he heard the hoarse whisper in Japanese coming out of the darkness. "Hey, gotta match?"

Ito relaxed. Sacho. Goddam Sacho. Always smoking. Never without a cigarette in his mouth. One day they'd bury him with one cigarette butt in his mouth and another up his ass.

Ito whispered, "Yes." He smiled, laying down his rifle and patting his jacket pocket for his lighter.

Sand kicked him in the back of the head, driving him forward and face down. Diving forward and straddling Ito's back, Sand lifted his arm high, bringing the elbow down hard in the spot he had just kicked.

The black Samurai stood up and moved away. There was no need to dismantle Ito's weapons. Sand knew this one was dead. Sand had heard his neck snap.

Salt's voice echoed in the darkened ape house, now lit only by his flashlight and the cigarette lighters of the three gunmen with him. "Now!"

On the other side of the cage, the noise came through the open slot behind Ford. An iron pipe beating on the bars and a man loudly yelling, "Hey, hey, hey!"

Ford had a queasy feeling in his stomach and he felt the pain knifing through his insides. Tension and fear. They were destroying him by inches. Salt was going to do it even faster and a lot sooner.

Over the yelling of the man and the beating of iron against the steel cage, Ford heard a screeching sound, followed by scuffling, then two dark shapes scampered through the open slot, moving on all fours, low to the concrete floor, their eyes bright with shock and uncertainty.

The door to the outside part of their cage slid down
behind them.

Baboons. Vicious killers.

Hideous, ugly, their doglike snouts twitching. Salt's flashlight beam pushed them back on the far side of the cage
away from Ford. The black sea captain cringed, his face
contorted with fright, both hands gripping the bars. Suddenly, stiffly, he moved away from the bars, until his back
was against the wall, facing the baboons.

He stared at the baboons, then turned to Salt. "For the
love of God, please! Let me out!"

"Told you, nigger, ain't nobody gonna touch you. 'Cept
maybe them two in there. Baboons can kill a man. Fact
is, they do it all the time in Africa."

Salt snapped his fingers, the sound carrying through the
room like a pistol shot. The three gunmen touched flame to
their rolled-up newspapers and moved closer to the cage.
"Three of you baboons in that cage," said Salt, "and one
of you better start tellin' me somethin'. Don't start lying
like a carpet, junglebunny, 'cause those neighbors of yours
can be mean."

He snapped his fingers again, and one man tossed his
flaming newspaper into the cage at the two baboons huddled in against a dirty wall. Both screeched and scurried
away, bumping into each other, bouncing off the bars.
Neither stopped their horrible screeching. One ran at
Ford, now backed into a corner. Turning his back to the
fear-crazed animal, Ford screamed.

Salt's fingers snapped twice more. The other two men
hurried forward, hurling their flaming newspapers into the
cage. Each man stepped back quickly, his eyes on the
baboons and the terrified black man imprisoned with them.

The added fire made them continue to screech, each
one pulling at the bars in fear and frustration. Killing
would be a release for them. One dropped from the bars
and, swiftly scurrying across the straw-covered floor of
the dirty cage, leaped at Ford.

Screaming, Ford used the strength of terror, pushing
with hands and feet, and drove the baboon back. But
the baboon—each weighed 90 pounds—didn't go far. He
crouched and moved sideways, his eyes bright with rage,
his ugly face glaring at Ford. Some of the straw was
catching fire, and smoke began to rise from the floor.

"I'm listening, nigger!" Salt's voice echoed throughout the huge concrete and steel room.

Ford stared at his bleeding hands, cut when the baboon's razorlike teeth had bitten into him. His Black Diamond mink coat had two long tears in the right side. The killer baboons now had an outlet for their fear and frustration.

The newspapers were burning out, but the two baboons were still ready to be destructive.

Salt's voice rang out again. "Got plenty of newspapers. Goddam plenty."

The two baboons moved toward Ford, their bright eyes burning into him. Blood oozed down the back of his hands as he pulled at the bars, leaving dark, wet patches where his hands touched the steel.

Salt's flashlight beam followed the baboons as they moved slowly toward Ford.

Kneeling on one knee in the darkness of the room, both hands gripping his .45, Robert Sand sighted and pulled the trigger. The roar from the powerful handgun echoed throughout the building. One of the baboons was lifted off its feet and into the air, slamming into a wall behind it, splashing blood against the stained gray wall. It lay dead while the other crouched over it in pathetic curiosity.

Sand was stomach-down on the concrete floor when he yelled "Freeze!"

No one moved. Salt's back was to Sand, the flashlight in his left hand.

"Face down where you are. Arms out in front. The flashlight. Place it beside you on the floor."

Salt did as he was told, saying nothing, making no moves. Like any Apache, he was no fool when it came to his life. The man behind him had shot good. One shot, one dead baboon. From the echo, it had to be a damn heavy gun. No, the Apache would wait.

But there were things he wanted to know about this man they had waited for.

Sand's commands were sharp. "Key to that cage, who's got it?"

No one answered.

Walking over to Salt, Sand looked down at the huge Apache, now face-down on the dirty floor. "I could find it myself."

Salt knew what that meant. "My back pocket."

Sand pressed the .45 hard against the back of the
Apache's head while his other hand fumbled for the key.
He found it. Picking up the flashlight, he backed off from
the Apache. As he moved away, he saw it. One of the
Europeans rolled over twice, trying to get into darkness,
his hand tearing at his shoulder holster.

Sand fired twice at the sound, spacing the bullets one
foot apart. The noise of the powerful handgun made the
remaining baboon screech.

Throwing the light where he had just fired, Sand saw
what was left of the man. His chest was almost entirely
blood-covered and he lay on his back, one foot drawn
up close to his crotch. He wasn't moving.

Sand's voice snapped at Salt, still lying flat, his head lifted
inches off the ground, staring at the man Sand had just
killed.

"Crawl!"

A corner of Salt's cruel mouth turned upward and his
eyes grew hard.

Sand's voice came out of the darkness behind the Apache.
"I want everyone together, where I can see them. Now
crawl and I won't say it again."

Salt's body tensed with white-hot anger. Made to crawl on
his face across a stinking, piss-smelling floor by a nigger.
By a goddam nigger! The Apache was livid. His huge
hands clenched into fists, opened, then clenched into fists
again. He crawled, every inch along the floor burning into
his brain.

Sand had crossed the room to the cage. Without a word,
he handed the key to Ford.

In seconds, the trembling, bleeding fingers of the black
ship's captain had opened the huge brass lock.

He stood next to Sand. Wiping his bleeding hands on the
side of his black mink coat, he breathed deeply and loudly.

"Get their guns," said Sand. The men lay side by side,
the flashlight beam covering them all. "Start with the
Japanese. I'll take *him*."

Sand meant the Apache.

Placing the .45 hard behind Salt's ear, Sand patted his
body. Salt carried a 9mm Walther P38, a German pistol and
a damn good one. Valbonne could afford the best.

"Got 'em," said Ford.

Salt, his face on the dirty floor, spat, his eyes hot with

hate. Even in his rage, he knew one thing. His men out-side had been taken by this son of a bitch. Three shots and no one had come. Not one fucking man. Damn, even the watchman had put up more of a fight.

Silently, Sand signaled Ford to back toward the door. With the flashlight still on the men face-down on the floor, Sand backed up too.

Ford backed up, then turned and ran toward the door.

Sand kept moving away from the men, the flashlight beam spreading into a wide, weakening circle of light. Switching off the flashlight and plunging the room into darkness, he turned and ran for the door.

Ahead of him, he heard Ford's car start. As Sand quickly ran through the door, the Apache's voice screamed from the darkness. "Niggah! You should have killed me!"

Sand didn't stop. Slipping into the front seat, he slammed the door, saying to Ford, "Move!" Then, notic-ing his bleeding hands, the black Samurai asked, "Can you drive?"

Smoothly, Ford pushed the engine into a loud, powerful roar, pulled away and sharply U-turned. Shifting gears, he sent the Mercedes speeding into the darkness. "What the hell do you think?" he yelled.

For almost a minute, they drove in silence, the powerful Mercedes roaring along the darkened road. Then Sand said, "Ease up. They won't be following. I took care of their cars."

"You knew. You knew it was a trap."

"I thought it might be."

"Why didn't you tell me? I mean what the fuck, Jack, I could have been killed back there."

"You weren't. And if I had told you, would that have stopped you from going after the $50,000? Would you have believed me? Haven't you closed your eyes to the truth since you've worked for Valbonne?"

Ford's lips were pressed tightly together. He inhaled deeply, then let the air out noisily. He said nothing. But he nodded his head twice.

Suddenly he braked the car, opened the door, and, with the motor still running, stepped out on the road. As the black Samurai watched, Ford took off his black mink coat and tossed it into a ditch.

Sliding back into the Mercedes, he slammed the door

and gunned the motor, the tires squealing as he speeded back toward Paris. "Coat reminds me of back there." He said nothing else during the entire drive back to Paris.

He didn't have to.

CHAPTER 10

Thoughts of Vengeance

"Forget the other assignments," said Valbonne. He was angry and uneasy without knowing why. Both of his small hands gripped the telephone receiver, squeezing until his knuckles turned white. "Return to Geneva, Mangas, as soon as possible."

The Apache said, "Sure 'bout that, Mr. Valbonne?"

"Yes, Mangas, I'm sure. What you've told me about our mysterious black friend who surprised you"—Salt's mouth twisted as the words slid into his ear—"well, I think he likes to travel, understand? We might be seeing him around here. I'd like you back to welcome him."

Salt's eyes were bright with hatred. Never in his life had he wanted revenge more than now. "Yes, Mr. Valbonne, I see what you mean. What about Saraga's men?"

"Two teams, Mangas. Divide them up, one or two of our men with them to guide them, to speak the language, things like that. Give the teams the list of· Paris assignments. I think we have two left, am I right?"

"Yes sir."

"Good. Let them take care of that. You return here. I think we'll be quite busy preparing for our friend and keeping an eye on certain other things. Understand?"

"Yes sir. 'Nother thing, Mr. Valbonne. Couple of Saraga's Japs don't speak English too good, but they tell me they may know this, this mysterious black man we've been running into. They don't know him personal, understand? But they've heard talk in Japan of somebody called the black Samurai, some black dude who's supposed to be something special when it comes to fightin'."

"Oh? Now that's interesting, Mangas."

"Yes sir. They've heard about him. He's supposed to be the only man, white or black, ever to be trained as a Samurai warrior, some kind of shit like that."

Valbonne was silent. Then he spoke softly. "Mangas, you must not underestimate our friend. If this man is the one spoken of in legends, then he deserves our utmost respect, especially since he's already proved himself."

Salt's mouth twisted, and he spat on the red-brick wall of the small gas station near the zoo. He had been taken by the nigger, humiliated, and now he had to listen to Valbonne get cute with words and remind him of the whole goddam thing.

"Mangas, you would do well to study the history of the ancient Samurai warrior. He was one of the best fighting men the world has ever seen. Swords, knives, hands, feet, stick, bow and arrow, horse—just about anything you can name, he mastered. You must know your enemy. Don't let him outfox you."

Salt took a deep breath, calming himself before he spoke. In a way, Valbonne was right. Coming unglued was not the answer. He was a full-blooded Apache, and no one was more cunning or deadly. No one. Not even the black Samurai.

"Don't worry, Mr. Valbonne, I'm gonna be a lot smarter the next time."

"Yes, Mangas. I know you are. About our project. Four more days and we're finished. It'll be shipped to Canada by our client. Six days after it leaves here, it'll be used."

Salt smiled into the telephone. "Good. What about the American piece of equipment?"

The trigger. The radar device that would set the bomb off.

"Completed. Finished and waiting in New York," said Valbonne.

"Way to go, Mr. Valbonne. I've got to set things up with Saraga's men here, but I should be able to head back in two or three hours. I'm looking forward to another meeting with our black friend."

Valbonne hesitated before he spoke. When he did speak, his words were gentle yet definite. "I'm certain you'll get your wish, Mangas."

The Baron placed his hand over the telephone receiver and looked at Robert Sand sitting calmly in front of him.

"Perrin says the whores are going out to Valbonne's place tomorrow."

The black Samurai nodded and said, "Tell him what to do."

Sand listened while William Baron Clarke, former two-time President of the United States, spoke long-distance to Otto Perrin in Geneva about whores. The plan was Sand's and he was betting his own life on it, plus the life of every man, woman and child in New York City.

The black Samurai wanted Perrin to do two things: hire a whore to do a specific job, and make one phone call to Valbonne sometime in the next 24 hours. Just two things.

With an hour before the Paris dinner in his honor, the Baron was dressed in tuxedo, blue shirt, black velvet tie. His wife was at the shop of a top Parisian hairdresser who charged $100 an hour. A Secret Service man— Frank Pines, the only other man who knew the relationship between the Baron and the black Samurai—had been ordered downstairs to listen at the hotel switchboard. Like Sand, the Baron was cautious.

Clarke hung up and turned to the black Samurai. "By a thread, son. Your black ass is gonna be out there by a thread."

"No choice. Ford's finished as an informant. Berk is the key. We've got to reach him. Who else can get closer to Berk than a whore hired by Valbonne? All she does is what she's told. She doesn't even have to say a word. If she's successful, we've got something to go on. And Perrin, from him just that one phone call."

The Baron frowned. "You're going into this thing depending on other people. I know how you work, and that ain't the way."

"No time. Ford now thinks Berk's right where Valbonne can reach out and touch him. Berk must be where the bomb is. Holz isn't much use to Valbonne, according to your Dr. Perrin. That leaves Berk. These facts, and that ski lodge being built by Valbonne, plus other men Ford saw at the chateau, and you've got something worth checking out."

"Ain't no tellin' who Valbonne's paid off in the Swiss police and local politicians. Can't trust nobody these days."

"That's why I prefer to work alone except as a last

resort. I don't doubt Valbonne's bought whoever he needs in Geneva, and he doesn't even have to tell them why. The Swiss love money and that's enough for them to do anything for it. There's also the chance we could be wrong and a show of force would scare Valbonne off and into hiding. There's also the chance that a bunch of people rushing the door would start shooting holes in the bomb and that would cause a problem, too. No. My life's on the line, so it'll be my way."

The Baron began to pace back and forth across the gold-colored carpet. "They'll be expectin' you, especially after that get-together at the zoo. Doctor at the American Hospital says Ford's got to have eight shots in the ass. Didn't know a baboon could be that damn dangerous."

"They can. I think it's just a precaution. Beats being dead."

The Baron stopped pacing and walked over to a large brown wood desk topped by a clean green blotter. Sitting down, he hurriedly wrote some names and addresses. When he finished, he stood up and walked back to Sand. "This here's somethin' else to go on. First name's my banker in Geneva. I'll call him and let him know you're on the way. I got $50 million on deposit there and I hope to hell you ain't leanin' toward spendin' it all. He'll give you what you need. There's also Otto Perrin's address and phone. Last one's the hotel where Zoraida Mahon's gonna be stayin' as of tomorrow."

"Got a photograph of any of these people?"

"All three." The Baron walked back to his desk, found the snapshots, and put them in a white envelope. He walked over to Robert Sand and handed him the envelope. "When you headin' to Geneva?"

"Now." Sand stood up, gripping the small Samurai sword with its 22-inch blade in its silver-and-black scabbard. "No reason to go to my hotel. This is all I own. I've got all my passports and almost $2,000 in American money. Take care of the hotels, will you?"

The black Samurai always checked into more than one hotel or room, each under a different name. A trick of the medieval Japanese warriors and spies. The Baron would pay the Paris hotel bills and set Geneva hotels under prearranged names.

"It's an hour's flight to Geneva. Can your banker friend get me weapons?"

"Money talks. He can get you an elephant for your bathtub if you need it. About Zoraida. She's deliverin' money to Valbonne tomorrow. Ganai packaged it for her. Four million dollars, American. Four suitcases. Three men will be with her, Saraga's goons. Valbonne sometimes meets her at the airport, or at one of his banks. Sometimes at her hotel. Either way, they'll get together almost as soon as her plane touches down. This is the last payment she's due to carry. She could be killed after that if Valbonne's covering his tracks. Big payment, the $50 million, is busting Ganai's ass, but he's swinging it for Saraga. That's got to be ready in about four days."

Sand frowned, his mind racing. "Four days? If the money leaves Japan in four days, that means Valbonne's got it shortly after that. It looks as though that bomb is due to go off around ten days from now. Valbonne's almost got it finished. Bet on it."

The Baron shook his head as though he had been kicked in the stomach and needed air. "We can't let him do that, son. We can't. Not to my country, no sir, we just can't."

His voice was strained and his eyes bright with tears he fought to keep back. He loved America, in the straight, uncomplicated way a simple man always loves anything.

Robert Sand stared at him, and for a second, a thought flashed across his mind. America and Japan. The two countries of Sand's existence, and he had to go against one to save the other. Or did he?

He told himself that maybe it wasn't that way at all. Maybe he was just going against men, not countries. It sounded better.

He walked toward the door, then stopped to look at the sad-faced Texan standing in the middle of the room, who suddenly looked every day of his 64 years. The Baron cared about America in a way few men ever had.

Sand said, "I'll do the best I can." That was the way of the Samurai, and for Robert Sand, there would never be another way as long as he lived.

Trembling with cold and excitement, Valbonne walked beside Salt in the snow. Both men wore huge dark glasses against the reflection of bright sun on soft white snow.

At noon, the glare of yellow sun on white snow pierced the naked eye like a needle.

Valbonne, wrapped in a $30,000 white ermine coat, rubbed his brown-leather-gloved hands together rapidly. When he spoke, his breath was steam in the cold mountain air. "Brighter than a thousand suns, Mangas. That's what the explosion will look like. I'm *almost* sorry I can't be in New York to see it."

The huge Apache chuckled. "Stay here, Mr. Valbonne, and count the money. When that baby goes off, ain't nothing gonna be breathin' or crawlin' anywhere near it."

The two men were walking alone in the snow-covered valley. Behind them, gray smoke floated up from a chimney of the snow-covered ski lodge, where outlaw scientists worked almost around the clock to complete the deadly package ordered by a vengeful Japanese soldier.

In front of them, the Apache's keen eyes watched the small brown wooden shacks used by armed guards. He turned to look behind him, watching the movements of six men "working" casually around the ski lodge. The "workmen" carried pieces of wood, or carpenter's tools, or other objects used in construction. Each "workman" was a paid killer, a man who asked no questions about killing except who and how much.

Each carried a handgun under his overcoat or thick jacket. And each knew exactly where a submachine gun or an automatic rifle was hidden nearby. Anyone near the men would think he was watching a work party. If the observer moved closer or tried to enter the ski lodge, he would learn he had made a fatal error.

Valbonne clapped his gloved hands together. "Ah well, Mangas, yesterday was yesterday. Today is a new world, is it not?"

"I still want him, Mr. Valbonne. Bad."

"That's good, Mangas, but do not allow your rage to blind you."

"It won't, sir."

"Good. Now, let's see. This afternoon, you're going into Geneva, right?"

The Apache nodded. "Eight men. Two will bring the whores back, the other six will be with me and the money."

"Good." Valbonne was careful. His men always drove the women out to the chateau and back to Geneva. It made security that much easier. That's why tape recorders were in the bedrooms. He had enjoyed some of the conversations, just as he enjoyed watching Mangas in bed with three women. That was Valbonne's pleasure and prerogative, to know every inch of the lives of those working for him."

"Mangas, be careful." Valbnnne didn't have to say more. "Be careful" meant come back with the $4 million, the last installment on the $50 million down payment. "I doubt if the whores are in danger," said the Frenchman, smiling as he spoke. "But I do think $4 million might be a temptation."

The Apache's face was hard and unsmiling. "Mr. Valbonne, I'd give a lot to have him try it."

"Good, good. This will be the last time the scientists will be taken from the ski lodge down to the chateau. Today I hope they indulge their sexual appetites to the fullest. After today, they'll work, eat, sleep in the lodge until the bomb's complete. I'm having beds brought in this afternoon. The sooner we finish, the better."

"Makes sense, Mr. Valbonne."

"Thank you, Mangas. I'm not inviting you to join the scientists and the whores today, because I want you concerned with security until this matter is complete."

"I understand, Mr. Valbonne."

"Good. Now, let's walk awhile. The cold makes me think and it clears my head."

"Whatever you say, Mr. Valbonne." The Apache had no thoughts for the cold and the snow or the beautiful snow-covered valley around him. He had no thoughts for the deadly creation being assembled in the ski lodge behind him. His thoughts were for the black Samurai, and they were thoughts of vengeance and hatred.

"Oh, Mangas, one more thing."

"Sir?"

"The girl, Zoraida Mahon. She's to be killed. I suggested it by way of slicing off all loose ends. Saraga agrees."

"We handle it?"

"No, his men will, the ones who came to Geneva with her and the money."

"Makes sense. What the hell."

Valbonne smiled. The Apache always understood killing.

CHAPTER 11

Zoraida

11:25 at night.

Two hours after walking out of the Baron's Paris hotel, Robert Sand walked into Geneva's Cointrin Airport. His muscles tensed with chill under his thin dark-blue raincoat. After changing $500 American money into Swiss francs, he asked for Swiss coins and walked toward a telephone booth.

The banker's name was Ludwig Gryff, and over the telephone, his German accent was cold and without emotion. Like all men dealing in big money, Mr. Gryff was polite, cautious, and used as few words as possible. "Yes," he hissed in a soft voice, "I was told to expect you, Mr. Williams." Sand was traveling under a passport reading Joseph Williams, a hardware salesman from Illinois.

Mr. Gryff tried a quick test. "Did our friend have on his cowboy boots tonight?"

Sand's reply was direct. "He wore a tuxedo, Mr. Gryff, because there was a dinner in his honor two hours ago in Paris. It was hosted by the widow of Charles de Gaulle. The dinner was held at a small villa outside of Paris given to the Empress Josephine by Napoleon. Each guest went through three security checks before being allowed inside."

Mr. Gryff chuckled, but not for long. "I had to make sure."

The dinner's location was a secret for security reasons, and the number of security checks was not to be revealed until the guests' arrival. Only the Baron or those close to him would have known this.

The black Samurai wanted no more tests. He took

91

charge immediately, his voice commanding and direct. "Mr. Gryff, I'm taking a bus into Geneva. That gives you one hour to obtain some items for me."

The German banker had worked for William Baron Clarke before and knew enough to respect the tough Texan and not to ask questions. He was well paid to do what he was told. "Please tell me what you want, Mr. Williams."

"First, please get all of the keys to my hotels. The Baron instructed you to make three reservations for me. Next, I'll need an American handgun, a Colt .45 ACP Commander, two grenades, two flares and a submachine gun. Each gun is to have two clips of ammunition."

Mr. Gryff's voice was natural and as unruffled as if he had just been asked for two paperclips and a rubber band. "I recommend the Swiss 9mm Parabellum Model 41/44. It has a 40-round magazine, easily detached if need be. This will cost the Baron quite a lot."

"Thank you, Mr. Gryff. One hour, in a car, front of the bus terminal. Just you."

"How will I know you?"

"I'll know you, Mr. Gryff." The black Samurai hung up, then dialed Otto Perrin's number. As the telephone rang, Sand turned to stare out at the darkened airfield.

Twelve hours later, Otto Perrin said, "Have you been to Geneva before?"

Sand swallowed the cool milk, emptying the glass. Placing it down on the silver room-service cart, he said, "Yes, twice. It was part of my education." Let Perrin guess the rest. It had been the Baron's idea several years ago to have Sand leave Japan for a few weeks each year, traveling to major cities, in preparation for their association. Sand gained knowledge, polish, sophistication. He also looked over the battlefields, because the missions he and the Baron selected would be fought in these cities.

That was also when the black Samurai and the former President of the United States pored over files, informants' tips, photographs and background on dangerous men, men who abused power and used it for themselves. Yes, it was an education, but nothing Robert Sand discussed with anyone. Secrecy was survival.

He said to Perrin, "When do the women go out to Valbonne's chateau?"

"In two hours."

Sand rubbed his unshaven jaw. He had slept well, but the Swiss didn't believe in overheating hotels. He could have used an extra blanket.

Two hours from now. He had phoned the airport and learned that Zoraida Mahon's plane had landed over an hour ago. That meant she was at the Hotel Waage on Lindenstrasse. With the whores at the chateau, that meant Zoraida would not be going there. Meaning, Valbonne would pick up the money from her at the airport or at her hotel.

Sand stood up and moved toward the bathroom to shave. He had checked into one hotel last night, gone up to his room, then left the hotel unseen and checked into another under the name Georg Elliot. He said to Otto Perrin, "Did you make all the arrangements as ordered?"

"Yes, but I don't see why we have to go to all that trouble. Can't I just say I'm leaving, then stay out of Valbonne's way?"

Sand turned and looked at the tall blond man. For a few seconds, the black Samurai said nothing. Then, "Doctor, did the Baron tell you how many men Valbonne's killed or tried to kill in the past three days?"

"Well, uh, no, no he didn't."

"Doctor, if he finds out what you've done, he'll kill you. It's not a question of you staying out of sight. After you make that phone call, you were told to leave Geneva by the following night. Permanently, doctor. Permanently."

The blond-haired man's lips twisted right, then left, and he nervously wiped the palms of his hands on his thighs. He was sitting down, but now he found it impossible to stay still. He stood up. "Look, I don't think I have to leave. I mean, I can't leave just like that. Do you have any idea what you're asking me to do?"

"I'm asking you to say alive. You're going to phone Valbonne and tell him that the tests you ran on blood samples from Peter Holz show possible infectious hepatitis. You're going to tell Valbonne that everyone near Holz must be inoculated. You're the man who's going to lure those scientists out of that ski lodge tomorrow night and down to the chateau. That's enough to get you killed."

"W-w-what? I don't understand. What's going to happen next? Why could that one telephone call get me killed?"

Sand rubbed his own neck with his hand. The phone call was to lure the scientists out in the open. Sand then planned to grab Berk. If he couldn't take him away from Valbonne, then he would kill him and as many of the other scientists as possible. How could he tell this to a man dedicated to saving life?

Besides, Sand never discussed his plans unless absolutely necessary. Secrets did not travel well. And only the dead could be counted on to listen quietly and never speak.

"Take my word for it," said Sand, "that phone call will tie you into something certain to be dangerous to you. Already you know enough to make you a danger to Valbonne."

"He doesn't know that."

"Doctor, only a fool underestimates his enemy. Don't you be a fool. Valbonne's a murderer, and there's a lot at stake here. A lot of money, a lot of lives. After today, you can't just lock your door and hope to keep on living."

Perrin licked his lips. "My practice, my friends, I—"

"The Baron will set you up in practice anywhere you want."

"Yes, well, I—"

The black Samurai watched the blond-haired man struggle with himself. Like Otis Ford, Perrin was not the type to let go. "Make the call now, doctor."

Dazed, Perrin walked slowly toward the telephone.

"Not from this room, doctor. That could cause us both trouble, if Valbonne starts to check. Leave the hotel, then call him. Tell him your reason for seeing everyone tomorrow is that you're leaving late tomorrow night to visit relatives in Sweden. He won't want to bring a new doctor in on such short notice. I suggest you cover yourself by making a plane reservation to Sweden first, then call Valbonne."

"You think of everything, don't you?"

"I try to. When are the women coming back?"

Perrin looked at his watch. "The madame told me she was being paid for four hours. They should be back in Geneva early this evening."

Sand said, "What's our girl's name?"

"Maria. Italian with big tits, the kind Berk likes. She says he practically walked on heads to get to her the last time she was out there. She doesn't know what's going on."

"Good. I hope she knows she must also pair off with him this time."

"She does. She says Valbonne makes them leave their purses behind downstairs. Clothes, too. The girls all pair off and go to the rooms naked."

Sand chuckled. "Valbonne's making sure no one has anything on them they shouldn't. Like a weapon or a tape recorder. Smart man."

Perrin smiled for the first time in minutes. "If he only knew. Whose idea was it for Maria to go about it in just that way?"

"Mine. Go make your phone call, doctor. Remember, *not* here, and make the flight reservations first."

Perrin was silent.

Outside in the hall, he pressed the elevator button and jammed both hands into his dark-brown fur jacket. Damn! Leave Geneva after working hard as hell to set up a practice. And all because some stranger, a black man, told him to. Well, we'll see about that. Impatient, anger heating within him, he again jabbed his thumb viciously at the elevator button.

Salt began wrapping a light-green bathtowel around the brown-and-black Soviet 7.62mm AK assault rifle, one of the most accurate submachine guns in the world. His voice was a steel command. "Let's go."

Two men each picked up two suitcases of money, each man carrying $2 million. Salt and three other men finished wrapping their Soviet submachine guns in towels and pieces of cloth. The Apache nodded his head toward the door. Two men opened it and stepped into the hallway, standing back to back. One signaled for Salt and the others to come out.

The Apache came through first, his hard eyes flickering from one end of the empty hall to another. He motioned the others to follow him. They did, each man with the wrapped weapon cradled in his arms. When Salt and his men were all in the hall, he turned and looked at Zoraida Mahon.

The tall, black-haired Spanish-Irish woman stared back at him, a cynical smile playing on her mouth. She was afraid of him, but didn't want to show it. His eyes sliced into her, and she felt a chill as though a death sentence had just been passed upon her.

Saraga's men, three Japanese bodyguards who had traveled with her from Tokyo, stood near the door, their slant-eyed, smooth yellow-skinned faces expressionless. They stared silently at her. Her hands smoothed down the front of her powder-blue suede skirt, and she took her eyes from the huge Apache to stare down at her black boots. When she looked up, he had gone.

One of the Japanese closed the door, and all three stood with their backs to it, each staring at the tall, beautiful girl. She looked from one to the other, leaning her head to the side in easy curiosity. She had known two of the men for the three years she had been with Saraga.

What was wrong? She felt uneasy. She smiled, clapping her hands together, then stamping her feet like a child out of school. She spoke in Japanese. "Well, that's finished. Hey, come on, what's wrong? Loki, Jana, hey, why the long face? Smile? We've done it. We're finished."

The three Japanese moved slowly toward her. One reached inside his pocket and took out a small bottle.

Zoraida began backing up, her hands lightly touching her throat. Her eyes were bright with fear.

The door to the stairway closed, but Robert Sand did not move. He continued to look through the slightly cracked door of his luxury suite, his eyes on the white-and-green door Salt and five armed men had just walked through with $4 million.

Of the three hotel suites booked for him in Geneva, one had been in the Waage Hotel on the same floor as Zoraida Mahon. Without saying why, this order had been given to Ludwig Gryff, and like delivery of the guns, flares and grenades, Mr. Gryff had produced.

With split-second timing, Sand had arrived on that floor less than two minutes before Salt and his armed men had come up the stairs to collect the money. The two Japanese guards in front of Zoraida's rooms had stared at Sand, but all they saw entering the room was a black man wearing dark glasses, gloves and a tan pile jacket, his face half hidden behind skis. Normal for Switzerland.

Sand had dropped the skis on the bed, taken off the mask and dark glasses, then moved to the door, cracking it less than an inch, in time to see the door opposite him open and the huge Apache step out into the hall.

Now Salt had left. After a two-minute wait, Sand

tucked the .45 in his waistband at the small of his back and stepped into the red carpeted hall. Seconds later, he stood near Zoraida's door, listening. Suddenly his head snapped closer to the door as his keen ears caught the sounds of a life-and-death struggle.

He heard a woman start to scream, then the sound was cut off, as though a hand covered her mouth. There was the sound of a chair crashing into a table, then a thud as something fell to the carpeted floor.

That's why the Japanese hadn't come out. They had a mission. They were carrying out orders to kill Zoraida Mahon.

Sand stood up straight, took a deep breath, then pressed the door buzzer, keeping his finger on it. In Japanese he said, "I have a message from Saraga."

Silence. He took his hand from the buzzer. He bent his knees slightly, his hands now at his sides, his fingers flexing quickly. Feeling fear was normal and the mistake was giving in to it. Sand willed himself into control of his fear.

He heard the lock click, then the door opened cautiously. Bending his knees deeper, he rammed his shoulder into the door and drove it open, smashing it into the man attempting to peek out at him.

The man went backward fast, then sat down on the red rug. Sand was inside the door, all motion, stopping for nothing. Reaching the man on the floor, the black Samurai kicked him in the face, his heel crushing the Japanese's nose into purple pulp.

In a flash, Sand took in the scene in front of him. One man was holding Zoraida, his hand over her mouth, his other arm pinning her arms to her waist. The other Japanese held a small bottle with a colorless liquid in his right hand, his left hand reaching out for Zoraida. Both men looked as though killing came easy to them.

The killing was to be done by that bottle.

With the speed and power he had developed in years of brutal Samurai training, Sand went into action.

His quick eyes caught the movement of the Japanese with the bottle, who dropped it to the red carpet and began clawing at his belt for an 8mm Nambu pistol. The other Japanese was trying to push Zoraida away from him, so he could deal with this intruder.

Leaving his feet in a dive, Sand flew through the air

as high as he could, turning his body sideways and smashing into the two men and the woman with his chest and legs, knocking them all backward into a table, chair and two yellow floor lamps. All four now crashed to the floor in a noise of broken glass, wood and human bodies.

Sand was on top. And he knew that men sent to guard $4 million carried guns.

In less than two seconds, the black Samurai smashed his elbow twice into the face of the man who had held the small bottle, bringing the elbow across, then back into the man's jaw. Blood oozed out onto the man's mouth, and he opened it to show broken bits of red-covered teeth.

Sand's head snapped toward the man who had been holding Zoraida. His hand now held an 8mm Nambu pistol, but the woman, now unconscious, was lying across his chest, preventing him from bringing the gun up high enough to use it.

He used his feet instead, kicking at Sand's balls, missing but sending pain deep into Sand's thigh. Pushing the pain from his mind, the black Samurai rolled on top of the man and smashed his wrist with the knife edge of his right hand. The man grunted, dropping the pistol, but his left hand came up for Sand's face, fingers clawing at the eyes.

As Sand leaned his head back from the deadly fingers, the man viciously shoved the unconscious woman from him, then drove his left knee into Sand's side, in a powerful attack to the ribs.

The black Samurai felt the wind go out of him, and he rolled off the man in the direction of the kick, not fighting the attacker's strength, but going with it, trying to avoid some of the power. His ribs pained him and his mouth was opened wide, desperate for air.

Rolling clear, Sand spun around to face the attacker just in time. The attacker was swift. He was standing, and when Sand spun around, he had only a fraction of a second to cross his hands quickly at the wrists and block a vicious kick aimed at the back of his head.

He blocked the kick, jamming the man's ankle, grabbing it, then pulling it up and to the side as hard as he could. As the man's balance weakened and he hopped to keep from falling, Sand yanked harder, then dropped the leg and threw himself forward, his right fist driving hard into the man's balls. He heard the man groan and curse in Japanese.

The black Samurai didn't stop to see if that was enough. Refusing to let the pain in his side grab at his mind, he willed himself to move faster, to execute his techniques with the precision he had practiced for years with his Samurai brothers.

Even scrambling to his feet, Sand made every move count, wasting neither time nor motion. As he stood up, he drove a right-hand backfist to the attacker's head, catching him high on the cheekbone. Swiftly pulling his right fist back, Sand swung it up and under the man's chin, snapping his head back.

The man staggered backward, arms clawing at the air for balance. No mercy would be asked or given in a deadly fight like this. Having trained in the East, both fighters understood this. Stepping in closer, Sand turned his body sideways, then powered a thrust kick to the man's stomach, extending his left leg as far as it would go, the foot tense and rigid when it reached the man's flesh.

The kick had everything. The power of Sand's leg from foot to hip, total concentration and a determination to survive. The attacker shot across the room, landing in a brown wooden chair, taking it with him crashing to the floor.

Swiftly, Sand spun around, his eyes sweeping the room. Zoraida moaned. The three attackers lay on the floor amid broken furniture and fallen lamps and flowers. As Sand bent over the woman, a gray-haired American couple, passing by the opened door, stopped.

The woman wore a bright-orange parka with a red scarf over her blue-tinted hair. The man was dressed in a white ski jacket and a commodore's cap. Both stared at the room, then down at the unconscious Japanese attackers lying across the broken furniture.

The black Samurai, huddled over the moaning Zoraida Mahon, looked at the old white couple and said gently, "Wild party. Mom sent me to get sis and bring her home."

The old lady in orange made a tsk-tsk sound with her thin wizened lips and said, "Alfred!" Without looking at the man, she moved from sight of the door. He took one more look at the room and at Sand, then followed her.

Americans. Sand shook his head. He gently tapped Zoraida's face. "How do you feel?"

She looked at him, her eyes glazed. "Like somebody's trying to tell me something."

Sand smiled. She had a sense of humor. He liked her without knowing her. "Get your purse and anything else. We're leaving."

She winced, closing her eyes and feeling her head.

"No time," he said, pulling her to her feet.

Her knees buckled. He held her up.

"I've got to call Sa—" She started to say the name, then looked at Sand.

"Don't bother calling Saraga. It was his idea to have them kill you."

Her green eyes grew large as she stood in the middle of the wrecked room, with both hands on her head.

"I'll explain as we leave," he said. "How do your legs feel?"

She stared at him, then looked down at her legs, and back at him.

Sand smiled. "Your legs look fine. Let's go. Eight flights down is a long walk. If you're thinking about the elevator, forget it. That old couple has probably told everybody that something bad for tourism is going on in this room."

She moved toward the closet. Stopping, she turned to look at Sand. "Saraga?" Her voice was high, and she frowned when she said it.

"Yes."

"Tell you something," she said. "It doesn't surprise me a goddam bit."

They were out of the room in less than 30 seconds.

CHAPTER 12

Target Date

Ian Berk, his bandaged left hand resting on his naked thigh, sat on the orange quilt-covered bed, staring at the voluptuous naked prostitute.

Maria Bonetti, 23 years old and a working whore since she was 14, was across the room, her bare back against the bedroom door. The tip of her pink tongue slid over her lips, wetting them. Her hands squeezed her large breasts, thumbs gently brushing the brown nipples.

Berk's right side ached from the beating of two days ago, but his chest rose and fell with his hunger for the Italian prostitute. His voice was hoarse with wanting her. "Here. Come here." He patted the orange quilt beside him.

Maria had a job to do, as instructed by Otto Perrin. Robert Sand had instructed Perrin.

Her pink tongue licked both of her thumbs, lightly covering them with spit. Then slowly, in small circles, she rubbed the spit into her brown nipples.

Berk whispered, "God!" His right hand urgently beckoned her to come to him.

Her voice was a moan and a whisper. "No, no, *caro*. No." She moved nearer to him, stopping just short of him, then both of her hands reached out to him, pulling him toward her as though by invisible wires. Berk smiled, a slave to the heat in his groin. He stood up and walked toward her, not noticing she was moving away, leading him on.

In seconds they were both in the bathroom, and Maria, with instinctive sexual cunning, let him touch her, his right hand sqeezing her breasts, first one, then the other. Then the hand slid to the small of her back, moving down to her ass, sliding along the curve.

Perrin had picked her for Sand's special job. He had picked well.

Berk's right hand went around her waist, pulling her near, the smell of her perfume mingled with the exciting natural smells and warmth of her body. His mouth was opened, aimed at hers. She smiled, her arms stiffening against his bare, hairy chest, keeping him away.

Skillfully, one of her hands dropped to his crotch, gently cupping the stiffness there. Her other hand gently touched his eyes, and like a hypnotist, she pulled his eyes to her, making him follow her every move. The woman's small hand moved from his eyes back to her moist opened mouth, down over her large breasts, then to her stomach, and finally to the triangle of soft brown hair between her legs. Berk's eyes narrowed with intense, hot interest.

Then—

As he watched, her fingers slid easily into her vagina, circled once, and when she pulled her fingers out, she was holding a thin gold lipstick tube.

Berk's eyes widened in surprise and his mouth opened to say something. Swiftly, she moved the fingers of her other hand to his lips, closing them with a gentle touch. She nodded her thick, dark head of hair once toward the bedroom, as if to say that someone was listening.

The surprised British scientist, standing naked in the bathroom with the voluptuous Italian prostitute, looked down at the thin gold tube in the palm of her left hand. In the bathroom light, it gleamed with an added brightness from the wetness of her body. Again he opened his mouth to speak, and again her right hand touched his lips, silencing them.

He frowned, understanding nothing, wanting to know everything.

A thin yellow rubber band held a small black eyebrow pencil tight alongside the two-and-a-half-inch tube. As Berk watched in amazement, she took the eyebrow pencil and printed the word "Baron" on the gold-trimmed bathroom mirror. Her printing was awkward, like that of an uneducated child, but the message was clear.

Berk's heart pounded and he forgot about the naked woman.

He continued to watch her hand. In seconds, she had

printed "Tape Recorder" and then turned back to him, her black hair swirling about her face as she nodded her head toward the bedroom. Berk's head snapped toward the bedroom, then back to the naked woman.

Maria, remembering instructions, looked over his shoulder as if to see if they were being watched, then she said in a loud voice, *"Mi amor,* ohhh, ohhh!" The sound carried from where they stood into the bedroom. It was supposed to.

Her body blended into his, flesh on flesh, and they kissed, both staring wide-eyed at each other. Maria watched him to see what affect the last few seconds had on him. Berk watched her because while he had a good idea of what was going on, he wasn't sure if it was the *right* idea.

Eyes wide, her tongue shoved deep into Berk's mouth, Maria moaned. It had to look good, Sand had cautioned. Valbonne's dangerous. Maria hadn't been told about the danger or why she was doing this. She had been told she would receive $2,000 over what the madame would give her from Valbonne. Best of all, the madame wouldn't know about the money.

Two thousand dollars. For Maria, that was reason to do anything asked of her.

Moving back from Berk, she faced the bedroom and laughed loudly at it. "Oh, you are a lover," she said, her long red fingernails opening the thin gold tube and plucking a piece of paper from it. She handed the paper and eyebrow pencil to Berk, again cautioning him to silence with a gesture of her fingers. As he looked at it, she turned from him and grabbed a handful of toilet paper, wet it under the gleaming chrome hot-water tap, and began rubbing the black words from the mirror.

Sand's orders, via Otto Perrin. Toilet paper could be flushed, leaving no trace. Perrin had made Maria act out for him most of what she was now doing. Sand's orders.

Berk looked at the small piece of paper and raised both eyebrows. He was breathing faster with the excitement caused by what he read.

The first line: FROM BARON—STAY READY U GOING OUT.

Second line: A/B: WHEN FINISHED? DAY SHIPMENT

Third line: NY XPLO DAY, WHERE. TRIGGER?

Fourth line: MONEY 4 U/U.S. VISA

The sound of the toilet flushing tore his eyes from the paper. Maria sat on the black, fur-covered toilet seat, jiggling the gold handle up and down like a child with a toy, grinning at him. Her hand danced a line in the air, signaling him to write.

He licked the tip of the eyebrow pencil. She chuckled low and sensuous in her throat, her eyes flashing at him under her long, black lashes. When Berk looked at her, she continued chuckling, shrugging her shoulders. Even with tension gripping him and making his hand shake with nervousness, he caught the humor in her earthy, silent comment.

Smiling at her, he licked the pencil again and began to write.

When he finished, she flushed the toilet again, disposing of the eyebrow pencil and rubber band. She took the paper from him, rolling it up, then slipped it back into the thin gold tube. Then she stroked his crotch, standing close to him, her pick tongue sliding wet and hot into his ear. "We have something to do, no?"

Berk sighed, relaxing, smiling at her. He nodded yes.

Maria had been told that she must proceed as if nothing were out of the ordinary. For her, sex for money was not out of the ordinary.

Later, there was a knock on the bedroom door. She sat up in bed as the door opened and one of Valbonne's guards stood looking in at them. "Time," he said.

"One last kiss," she said and turned to Berk. Her hands pulled him to her and he rolled on top of her willingly, and as their tongues met, her hand, unseen by the guard, took the small gold tube from under the pillow.

As Berk and part of the orange quilt covered her, her right hand was hidden as it slipped the small gold tube back into her vagina.

"Hey, let's go!" The guard moved into the room, stepping toward the bed.

"OK, OK," said Maria. Leaping from the bed, the voluptuous black-haired prostitute, her face smiling like an innocent child leaving a sandbox, ran across the light-blue carpet in short, quick steps, her large breasts bouncing, her elbows tight against her sides.

The guard stared at her, then tore his eyes from her nakedness to smile at Berk. "Goddam lucky you are, fella."

At the door, Maria turned and waved to Berk. *"Ciao, amore."*

The door slammed behind her and the guard, leaving the bearded scientist alone in the room and in the bed. Suddenly, he felt cold and afraid.

Robert Sand spoke slowly and carefully into the telephone, his breath steaming in the twenty-degree Geneva night. He was speaking from a public telephone. Ten feet away, Zoraida Mahon sat in the front seat of a rented silver-colored Porsche, her face almost hidden by a white fur-trimmed parka and dark glasses, watching him speak long-distance to Paris. The Baron listened intently, a shrewd tactic developed during 40 years of fighting in the political jungle.

"Project finishes three days from now." Sand read from the small piece of paper in his hand. It had been passed on to him 15 minutes ago by Mr. Gryff, who in turn had passed an envelope containing $2,000 in Swiss francs and German marks to Maria Bonetti.

"Project ships from Hamburg, Germany, to Montreal. It'll be on a ship owned by the buyer. Project to be in use one week after leaving Europe."

The Baron drawled into Sand's ear. "Damn!" Then he asked, "Anything on where?"

"Note says 'Long Island subway aban.' I guess that means an abandoned subway on Long Island."

"Say which one?"

"No. Next to the word 'trigger' he's written 'Astoria.' "

"Means trigger and damn subway are both around there somewhere. They'll bring it to Astoria, to do whatever last-minute stuff's necessary, then slip it on down into that abandoned subway and cart it off somewhere. Doesn't say where, does it?"

Sand looked at the note again. "No, except for one thing. There's a capital E at the bottom of the page. Same handwriting as everything else."

"What you make of that, son?"

"Taking a quick shot at it, I'd say it could be the Empire State Building."

"Hot damn! Betcha you kicked it right between the eyes. Gotta be it, gotta be. They gonna put it under that tall sumbitch and that's all she wrote."

"Three days to finish, five days across the ocean, and the

two days from Montreal to Long Island to Manhattan. Tight schedule."

"Any thoughts?"

"Yes. First one is to get the people working on the project out into the open."

"Then what?"

"Eliminate them."

"Yes."

The Baron said, "Hmmmm. When?"

"Can't do it sooner than tomorrow night. That was the call you made to the doctor last night. He's set things up for tomorrow night. I can't get in, but if they come out, I might be able to—"

"Eliminate them."

"Yes."

"Good. The banker helpin' you?"

Sand smiled. "He doesn't tell many jokes, but he does what he's told. I've got the girl with me. They tried to hit her this afternoon."

"No surprise to us. Might have been one to her. How she holdin' up?"

Sand looked at her. She smiled at him and waved. "Fine. Nice sense of humor. Didn't seem too surprised when it happened. Says our Japanese friend is a hard case. I may need her help tomorrow night."

"Your play, son. Just keep an eye open for the Indian. He don't make too many jokes either. I'm staying over in Paris for a couple of days, until we get this thing cleared up. You think Berk's tellin' it straight?"

"Not sure. That's another reason for hitting the people working on the project. No matter what happens, there'll be no one around to finish it. There's no reason for Valbonne to doubt the doctor yet. The German is really ill and it could be catching. They'll come out tomorrow, I'm sure."

"Take care, son. Keep one eye on that Indian and one on your behind. I'll wait to hear from you."

Sand hung up.

In the Porsche, he turned to Zoraida and said, "Valbonne's probably looking for you. He might think you've left Geneva, but there's no sense in taking chances. I've got something to do tomorrow night, and I'd like your help. After that, I'll see that you get out and get a little money to get you started somewhere."

She grinned, most of her face hidden by the fur-trimmed hood of her parka and the dark glasses. "I'd be dead if it wasn't for you. Three years with Saraga, watching him pull every dirty deal under heaven and always thinking it was happening to someone else, not to me. Well, it almost did. I owe you. I owe Saraga, too."

"Thanks." Earlier, he had told her the truth about why Saraga'd used her as a courier, that it wasn't gold but blood the Japanese shipping magnate was after. Learning about plans to use an atomic bomb on New York City had shocked her more than the attempt on her own life. She had told Sand something of her life, but he had known most of it, anyway.

She was 26, intelligent, strong-willed, tall and pretty, once-divorced, and had spent one year of the three she had worked for Saraga as his mistress. She had met him when she was a journalist, and the money he offered her to work in public relations for him had been more than the $80 a week she was getting from a Dublin newspaper. A hell of a lot more.

From public relations to mistress had brought even more money, but it had drawbacks, too. She had become closer to his work and had begun to see things about him that separated them as man and woman. Even when she stopped sharing his bed, it had still been difficult to close her eyes to his increasingly far-right politics.

The money, however, made it bearable.

Until today.

"The Irish in me laughs about it, the Spanish in me wants to peel the skin off his balls."

Sand smiled and said, "Ouch!"

"Thanks for the parka," she said. "You're a good man in a fight or a plight. You haven't told me much about yourself. You don't look like a fairy godmother." Her eyes were hidden behind the dark glasses, but in the cold night her voice was rich and warm. "Come to think of it, you don't look like a fairy, either."

"You know my name."

"Robert, that's all. As they say in America, big fucking deal. One thing I know, you're the black Samurai Saraga's goons were talking about. I heard you speak Japanese before you tiptoed into the room."

Sand smiled at her. "You've a nice sense of humor and a way with words."

"I laugh to keep from crying. Sad to say, crying keeps you from laughing, too. It's a defense mechanism, like my direct and straightforward, occasionally foul mouth. Keeps people you don't like at the other end of your twelve-foot pole."

"And people you like?"

"I advise them to pray a lot. I'm fun but I can be hell."

"Thanks for the warning."

"Uh, will you do me one favor?"

He nodded.

"Don't speak a word of Japanese to me, please?"

Smiling, Sand turned the key in the ignition, and the Porsche's powerful motor roared to life. "Hungry?"

"For certain. And cold."

They had a delicious dinner at a French restaurant near a gambling casino ten miles outside Geneva. Over a large brandy, her eyes searched his face. "Robert, mysterious, mysterious Robert."

The fireplace was warm behind them, and a fat man who never stopped smiling played French songs on an old accordion. Sand said, "You knew nothing and you almost got killed. Knowledge can hurt. My life depends on no one knowing anything about me. I work alone, at least most of the time. Just accept that, please."

"Black Samurai." Her tongue flicked at the brandy glass, and her strong, beautiful face, with its green eyes, seemed to search his face for what he refused to tell her.

"I'll find you a place to stay."

Her green eyes sparkled in the firelight. "That's up to you." She leaned her head to one side, mocking him, challenging him without saying a word.

He was quick, too. He only nodded, his eyes locking hers. She was offering herself, and he would accept. Maybe she was feeling him out to see if he or anyone connected with him would be her next wealthy patron.

He understood this. It was a hard world and you got through it as best you could.

She appreciated style. He knew that. There was no need to say more.

CHAPTER 13

Apache Ways

When he opened his eyes, she was lying awake beside him, her shrewd green eyes searching his face. She lay on her left side, left hand propping up her head. He was lying on his side facing her, and his hand reached out to touch her hip, feeling the warm flesh under his fingers, then pulling her toward him. She slid closer, her hand reaching out to caress his face.

"Morning." Her voice was a sensual whisper.

"Night was OK, too."

"Only OK?"

"On a scale of one to ten, you were eleven."

She laughed once, low in her throat, and drew him closer to her, her warm arms tight around his neck, her long legs wrapping around and in between his. "You sure know how to keep harmony in the world."

He grinned. "We're in there trying."

She chuckled. "I'll say. More people like you and the world would bask in racial peace forever, or some kind of shit like that."

"You've helped me by telling me about the land and roads around Valbonne's chateau. I'll keep my promise. I'll get you out of Geneva and see that you've got money. But it'll have to wait until after tonight."

Her fingers gently traced the scars on his muscular brown chest, and she grew serious. "Tonight, will it be dangerous?" Her eyes moved to his face, then down to the scars being traced by her fingers. "Are these souvenirs of other nights?"

His hand left her firm hip and touched her head, losing itself in her dark brown hair, making slow circles in its softness. "It's a strange thing about fear. You never lose it. But you learn to live with it, to control and sometimes conquer it. Your mind is the key. If you let it be afraid, it will be. The trick is to control it, not let it control you."

"That answers my question. What if something happens to you? Where does that leave the unemployed Spanish-Irish princess?"

"If I come back, you'll be taken care of, maybe not in grand style, but you'll be alive, away from Saraga and with some money. If for some reason I don't come back, well, I guess that takes me off the hook for your future."

She kissed him gently, brushing his lips with hers, then leaning back and letting her green eyes swallow his face. "Come back," she said softly.

Robert Sand kept his thoughts to himself. Even if her concern wasn't for him but for what she thought he represented—money, power, freedom—he felt she was entitled to grab her own future. It was a hard world, and just getting through 24 hours of it took more than most people had. Let Zoraida Mahon survive as best she could.

"Cold town, Geneva," she said, "with people to match. Town's cleaner than a nun's conscience, but all they live for is money. Cold, cold, cold." She pressed herself closer to him, her face in the warmth of his neck, feeling the strength of his arms around her. They lay that way quietly, each thinking of the future and survival.

"No, I figure he hasn't left Geneva, Mr. Valbonne." Salt's huge hand gripped the eight-inch black-leather-wrapped wooden handle of his 30-foot bullwhip, swinging it overhead in wide, noisy circles, each turn of the whip making a loud whoosh. Suddenly, the Apache snapped his wrist forward and the ugly whip flew straight ahead swiftly, chopping a snow-laden branch from a tree. The branch fell from the tree as though it had been neatly sawed off, the white snow plopping softly on the snow-covered ground in front of them.

The two men were again in the small valley near the ski lodge, standing alone in the snow and quiet around them.

"I tend to agree with you, Mangas, judging from past

patterns. Our black Samurai knows just where to go. I feel strongly he's going to hit us, but I'm not sure where."

Salt snapped the whip again, the crack echoing in the stillness of the white, cold outdoors. His breath was steam as he spoke. "Can't get near this place, not even him. Guards outside the building, inside, too, and they got orders to blow shit outta anybody that ain't you and me."

Valbonne, his hands jammed deep in the pockets of his white ermine coat, said, "You sound as though you are beginning to respect this black Samurai." His keen eyes watched the Apache, who stared straight ahead. Drawing back his wrist, Salt again drove the whip at the tree, sending soft white snow flying in all directions.

"He's a fighter, Mr. Valbonne, I'll give him that."

Valbonne chuckled. "One would say, Mangas." The Frenchman moved in place to keep warm, his breath white, then disappearing in front of his face. "Three men in Miss Mahon's suite couldn't handle him. I wonder what he plans to do with her? Fortunately, there's nothing she can tell him about the bomb. Only about the money. Still, I get the feeling that he knows what he's after, not just the small targets but the big one as well. I can almost sense this is a thinking man, quick but not impulsive, brave but not foolish. Seems almost a sacrifice to blow his brains out."

The Apache's face went hard with hatred and perhaps jealousy, something he would never admit to Valbonne. "Yeah," he muttered. "He thinks." The whip flew forward again, the crack echoing like a rifle shot, driving snow high into the air from a short, squat tree.

"Oh, Mangas, about bringing the scientists from the ski lodge tonight, I—"

The Apache's head snapped toward him. "What's that, Mr. Valbonne?"

"Slipped my mind. So much to worry about. Dr. Perrin called, said Holz might have hepatitis and that everyone should be inoculated just in case. I'm bringing the men from the ski lodge tonight. Perrin will be at the chateau and—"

The Apache, his eyes narrowed to slits, interrupted. "I don't like it, Mr. Valbonne. No way. Somethin', some-thin'—I just don't know. Apache ways, I guess."

Valbonne stared silently at the huge Indian. When he

spoke, his voice was soft. "I respect your opinion, Mangas. Keep talking." The Frenchman's face was red with the chill, and to keep warm, he lifted first one foot, then the other off the ground repeatedly as Salt spoke.

"Well, I don't know. Perrin calls, the men come out of the ski lodge, and shit, that black dude's around, and well, I just don't know. You know that's an Apache trick. If you can't get in, get the other guy to come out. My people were damn good at getting soldiers to come out of forts and other places. In the old days, we'd let soldiers chase us, and when they had ridden a ways, they found out they had ridden into a lot of bad-ass Apaches hiding somewhere, ready to cut their balls off."

Valbonne said, "Mangas, let's go back to the chateau. We have some telephone calls to make and some checking up to do. It may well be that you will have to make a house call to a doctor, dear Apache friend."

Forty-five minutes later, the two men sat in the large, luxurious main hall of Valbonne's chateau. Both were grim, unsmiling. They had made telephone calls, they had checked certain facts.

"The doctor is a liar," said Valbonne. "Thanks to you, we may well have avoided a serious setback in our plans to deliver the atomic merchandise to Mr. Saraga."

Salt held the rolled-up black whip in his right hand, gently tapping it against his faded blue jeans. "I'll go look up the good doctor and bring him out here. Him and me's gonna talk some."

Valbonne smiled. "I have faith, Mangas, that you will obtain answers Dr. Perrin never dreamed of giving."

"That ain't all, Mr. Valbonne. I think we oughta keep them men up at the lodge, just let 'em stay there and work their asses off like you had planned, you know? Now, when those two cars come along the road tonight to this place right here, there's gonna be a surprise for somebody. My men gonna be ready to kick ass, especially if it's black."

Valbonne smiled, nodding his head once in tribute.

Salt was quiet. Then, turning to the Frenchman, the Apache said softly, "Hey, Mr. Valbonne?"

"Yes, Mangas?"

"I think too, you know?" The words were those of a sad child seeking approval.

"Yes, Mangas. There can be no doubt about that now."

"No answer." Sand hung up the telephone, his eyes turning to Zoraida.

She shrugged. "So he took your advice. Didn't you tell him to leave Geneva?"

Sand walked to the window of his comfortable hotel suite and looked out at the cold Geneva darkness. He wore all black—turtleneck sweater, leather pants, work shoes. His Colt .45 ACP Commander hung butt down along his left side, in a black leather holster.

His hands toyed with his 27-inch Samurai sword, his prize won in the last competition among his Samurai brothers and presented to him by Master Konuma. He looked thoughtful. "Yes, I did. But I got the feeling he wasn't happy at the thought of pulling out. Still—"

He turned to face her, calm and relaxed as he looked at the woman, who chewed her bottom lip nervously and searched his face with her deep green eyes. "That's a beautiful sword," she said, more from a need to say something than from interest.

He was kind to her. "Yes, isn't it? It's the only thing I really own. It's all I have, and I suppose I keep it because of what it represents. It reminds me of what I should be, especially when I think of who gave it to me."

"You must tell me about that someday, if you want to."

She was no fool. She sensed how private a man he was.

"Perhaps," he said. In truth, it was unlikely he would ever tell her about the sword and how he came to have it.

"Time to go," he said. "Repeat the address to me once more."

She made a face, like a child being told to eat turnips. "I know it, you damn unbeliever."

"Repeat it," he commanded.

Slowly, her eyes looking at the ceiling in annoyance, she repeated the banker Ludwig Gryff's address. Sand had arranged for her to stay there.

"Good. Stay there until you hear from me."

"If I don't?"

"If you don't, you won't."

"Your sense of logic is overpowering." Her voice was cynical and she didn't smile. Suddenly, she stamped her foot as though being forced to do something she didn't want to do. Running to him, she threw herself into his arms, holding him tightly. She was tall, but still she stood on tiptoe, her breath warm in his ear, as she whispered, *"Cuidado, cuidado, mi hombre valiente."* Be careful, my brave man.

Pulling away, she turned her back to him. His hand reached toward her, then stopped.

He walked by her, the sounds of her gentle sobbing following him toward the door.

Otto Perrin lay naked on the cold gray concrete floor of Valbonne's wine cellar. His back was shredded, sliced into slivers of blood-red flesh by Salt's 30-foot black leather bullwhip.

For the lean blond doctor, the agony was excruciating. The Apache was a master of pain. First the bullwhip, snapping loudly, tearing into flesh, turning it into bloody strips, the snapping punctuating Perrin's high-pitched screams.

Then the gasoline, poured from a fifteenth-century silver goblet onto Perrin's open, bleeding flesh. The scream this time had been so loud that Valbonne winced, his face twisting at the high-pitched sound that seemed to be higher than any human being was capable of. When the gasoline touched his sliced, bleeding flesh, Perrin screamed inhumanly, flopping from side to side, finally writhing slowly, face down on the cold floor, his own blood dark beside him on the concrete floor.

"I think he'll do it now, Mr. Valbonne," said the Apache.

Valbonne, sitting near a large dark-brown keg of red wine, got up and carried a black-and-gold antique telephone over to Perrin, setting it down beside him on the concrete floor, careful not to set it in any blood.

"Really, Mr. Perrin," said the Frenchman. "You say you're leaving town by plane, but you make no reservation, nor have you even inquired about one. Your customary laboratory says it has not run any tests for you in ten days. Ten days! Now I ask you, Mr. Perrin, is that a nice thing to have us believe? And the woman—now there should be a lesson to you in the future. When you invite a woman to spend a few days with you in Lausanne, well, Mr. Perrin, Lausanne is a beautiful place, but it is not Sweden. It is Switzerland, not Sweden. So now, you call the man you say you have been working with, and you find out from this Mr. Gray where this black Samurai is. Will you do that, Mr. Perrin?"

Perrin opened his mouth. "Ahh . . . ahhh." He lay on his stomach, his blond hair wet with perspiration and blood, his eyes glazed with pain, his brain and body gripped by agony he never thought existed. Slowly, his hand inched toward the telephone.

Valbonne stood up, looked down at him, and smiled.

The Baron gripped the telephone receiver, his eyes narrowing, his mind racing.

He muttered to himself as well as to the operator. "Come on, goddammit, come on!" He had always been impatient. He was worse than that now. He was trying once more to reach Robert Sand and was having no luck. The telephone call he had just received from Otto Perrin had been more than enough to make him impatient. "Can't reach your man," Perrin had said.

"Well, why the hell should you," the Baron had replied. "That's his way. He wants you to know where his ass is, he'll tell you."

But Perrin had come back strong. "I think they're moving *it* out earlier."

Christ! The Baron had almost yanked the telephone out of the wall when he heard that.

"I think your man might want to check it out," Perrin said, sounding as though he had been hit by a tall building, but hell, the Baron had no time to check out anybody's health. Moving it out earlier!

The Baron, his hand over the receiver, had motioned to Frank Pines to get on the other phone and start running down Sand at the hotels and other numbers they had for him. Pines moved fast. Hotels first. Nothing. The Baron held on with Perrin.

Finally—"We checked every goddam number on him, but nothin'." The Baron knew where he might be. Somewhere in the cold darkness and snow of the Swiss mountainside, trying to kill seven men before they killed seven million. He wasn't telling the doctor that.

Perrin said, "Give me the hotels, so I can leave a message for him."

The Baron stopped breathing, his heart pounding. He had never told anybody where they could find the black Samurai. The black Samurai was always told where to find them. That had been the only way of handling a mission or an attack strike. But now—now!

William Baron Clarke thought of seven million people in the city of New York. An atomic bomb dropping on a city in the country he loved and had served for over 40 years.

He took a deep breath and let it out. He spoke slowly, his heart pounding, and not feeling good about what he was doing. Not good at all.

He gave Otto Perrin the three Geneva hotels' names and Sand's three aliases. Seconds later, the Baron hung up, his face ashen under his Texas sunburn. He walked to the window of his Paris hotel suite and stared out at the night. Frank Pines watched and said nothing.

CHAPTER 14

Slaughter in the Snow

The black Samurai stood in cold darkness, snow up to his ankles, letting the dry Swiss winter air gnaw at his face like a rat's teeth. He stood in the tree's shadow, away from nearby patches of pale-yellow moonlight. The cold burned his ears, seconds later quickly numbing them.

His left shoulder leaned against the tree's hard surface, the tan butt end of the Swiss Model 41/44 submachine gun balanced on his hip, his black-leather-gloved hand tight around the wooden grip behind the trigger. The gun, just over 30 inches long, weighed 11.4 pounds, had a 9.8-inch barrel and a 40-round magazine. Robert Sand had fired submachine guns in Tokyo, where he had spent time on the firing range with the crack bodyguards of the Emperor Hirohito. The guns were effective only up to 100 yards.

Sands was 50 yards away from the one road coming out of the ski lodge valley. He had confirmed that road's existence with the help of Ludwig Gryff. It was Gryff who had approached the Geneva office of building permits for information on 100 miles of land around Valbonne's chateau. Gryff, a respected banker, was known to advise potential real-estate investors and had no trouble getting what he wanted.

As far as Sand was concerned, his target tonight was anyone coming along that small road leading out of the valley where the land office had registered building permits on Valbonne's ski lodge. Gryff's information had revealed only one road in or out of that small valley. One road. One enemy. Sand waited.

The road, deeply snow-covered nearest the valley and

less snow-covered as it neared Valbonne's chateau, was shaped like an elongated horseshoe. One long end of the horseshoe led from the valley, the other long end led to the chateau. The rounded part of the horseshoe, a sharp turn in the road, was where Robert Sand waited in ambush.

He wore all black—form-fitting wool-line leather jacket reaching down to his hips, wool turtleneck sweater, leather pants, wool socks, workshoes. Under the jacket, a shoulder holster held his Colt .45 ACP Commander. A black canvas bag hung from his left shoulder. Inside were ammunition clips for the .45 and submachine gun. Also inside, its beautifully crafted black-and-gold handle sticking out of the bag, was his short sword. Two grenades were clipped to the left breast pocket of the leather jacket. Two red-colored flares stuck out of the right breast pocket. Robert Sand had been cautious. His car was hidden near the main road to Geneva, almost a mile away. He had given himself time, carefully making his way to the spot chosen for this attack on Valbonne's atomic scientists.

For almost 45 minutes, he waited in position, his superb Samurai training allowing him to stand motionless in the snow and darkness.

The waiting ended.

He heard it, the sound of tires crushing ice and frozen snow, the wheels slowly moving toward him in the night. The tree he hid behind was on a small incline, giving him the high ground. But he would still have to strike fast. Seconds after he attacked, his position would be a dangerous one.

The car sounds came at him out of the night, slowly, deliberately. His keen eyes didn't blink when the white, wide stripe of light from headlights slid along the snow far out in front of the car. He reached up to his head, pulling down dark goggles over his eyes, adjusting the cold rubber border to the bridge of his nose.

Headlights shining into the white snow didn't bother his eyes. The goggles were for the flares he planned to use.

For the first time in a while, he shifted his feet, feeling the cold numbness in his toes, but swiftly pushed thoughts of discomfort and fear from his mind. His heart beat faster than it had 30 seconds ago, and he opened and closed the gloved fingers of his right hand several times.

Twice he took a deep breath, letting it ease slowly from his lungs, calming himself, collecting all of his energies and reflexes, directing all of his strengths into what he had to do.

The black Samurai was ready.

His ears strained to pick up the sound of a second car. With at least seven scientists, there should be a second car, but he couldn't hear it.

The first car was in sight, a black shapeless mass in the darkness, its front bright with harsh white headlights. He shifted the submachine gun to under his left armpit and took a grenade from his pocket.

Pulling the pin, he drew his right arm back far and high, then lobbed the grenade through the darkness down at the car.

Still standing, he ducked behind the tree, turning sideways, steeling himself for the explosion. It came, a roar in the quiet night, flame and smoke rolling quickly out of the car through broken windshield and windows, through a motor with the hood blown off. Flying glass and pieces of hot metal disappeared into the snow on either side of the road, and a man screamed loudly a fraction of a second after the explosion.

The car slid sideways, its right side blocking the road.

Flames poured from the car, the red-orange fire crackling sharply in the night. Quickly, Sand stepped from behind the tree, the Swiss submachine gun gripped tightly in both hands, the butt pressed hard against his right side. The front door facing him on the side was bent in as though it had been hit hard by a speeding truck.

He saw the driver, his back crawling and alive with orange-blue flames, hanging through the empty space where the windshield had been blown entirely away. The driver was face-down in the engine and he wasn't moving.

The back door on the right side was open and a man hung out, lying on his back, mouth open and face covered with blood. Light from the crackling flames lit up his face and shredded clothes. Small wisps of steam rose from around him where flames and heat from his dead body met the snow.

Sand was about to fire the submachine gun when his finely honed reflexes made him stop. He could almost feel the hairs on the back of his neck stand up, and he grew tense with a feeling of danger, an awareness many Samurai over the centuries had developed with years of concentration.

The dead man lying out of the car on his back had both of his arms spread wide. The orange flames sent black shadows dancing across his body, and there was enough light to see the small radio held in his hands by a death grip.

A radio!

It was then that Sand heard another car speeding along the road, seeing its headlights moving silently, swiftly along the snow. Suddenly, the car stopped, and he heard the sound of doors opening, men shouting, boots hastily crushing snow and ice underfoot.

A trap.

He turned, crouching, hearing ugly, strange sounds of other machines coming at him in the night.

Behind him, snowmobiles, making a noise like giant power saws. Four of them, not close, but closing in, their lights small in the night, bobbing up and down over uneven ground as they relentlessly made their way through the snow and darkness toward him. He was in the middle —snowmobiles behind him, men from the second car in front of him.

That radio. It meant the second car and the snowmobiles were linked by radios, too. They had been expecting him. His face was grim, tense, his mouth a hard line of determination. Samurai. It was time to fight.

He turned to look at the burning car, now blackened and ugly, the flames low and almost gone. To go straight ahead meant moving closer to the ski lodge, closer to more of Valbonne's men.

He would go back, try to fight his way on foot through the snowmobiles and reach his car almost a mile away. He had to start now. There was no telling how many more men might be on the way, brought to this cold killing ground by a hand radio.

He moved from the tree, his strong legs, conditioned by hard daily five-mile runs in Samurai training, kicking up the snow. He stayed in the darkness when he could, quickly moving over open moonlit ground into shadows, crouching, stopping to listen.

Close behind him, men shouted and he saw flashlight beams move back and forth. Ahead of him, the noise from the snowmobiles grew louder, a harsh, ugly sound reaching for him out of the night. Soon he would be in the center of a small circle, a circle that would quickly tighten and crush all life from him.

Crouched in the darkness of a large tree, his right knee in the snow, the black Samurai decided to push the circle back.

He turned, facing the men on foot behind him, now moving toward him. They had passed the tree where he had stood and tossed his grenade. Bringing the Swiss submachine gun up to his right side, both hands gripping it tightly, he waited. Out of the darkness he had left a minute ago, two men trotted stiffly, awkwardly through the snow, rifles held across their chests.

He fired, the 41/44 jerking upward, his strong hands quickly holding it down, in place, on target. Hot empty shells leaped out from the gun, bouncing off his hands and forearms.

The two men fell backward, flopping in the snow, one turning over on his side. Their rifles flew upward as though the men had decided to throw the guns at targets overhead in the air.

Bending low, Sand turned and ran from the shadows, out into the moonlight, toward another tree. Shouts, then gunfire behind him, the bullets spraying snow close to his heels. He left his feet in a dive for the shadows and cover of another tree, landing short of it, crawling through the cool snow on his stomach until he reached it.

Just as he figured.

The gunfire drew the snowmobiles toward him. The noise of the machines grew louder, as they changed course and headed toward where he had fired from.

He heard shouts and curses in German, French and English.

Again and again, the word "submachine gun" was shouted out loud.

He prepared himself.

He had the grenade in his hand when he faced the sound of the snowmobiles. They were moving fast, lights going up and down. He quickly made out three of them almost side by side, slowing down over bumps, skirting the trees in their path. Three together. It was as good a target for the grenade as he might get all night.

He pulled the pin, his eyes on the machines bobbing up and down, his concentration as intense as it had been in training, as it had been when he won the antique Samurai sword in the last competition, before Master Konuma and Sand's Samurai brothers were slaughtered.

He counted to three, scrambled from the shadows and out into the moonlight. He tossed the grenade, watching its black shape arch in the night. He rolled back into the shadows and barely made it behind the tree when the explosion roared through the night, tearing apart men and machines. The ground shook under him and the orange flash from the grenade lit up the darkness.

He heard the screams, the agonized cries, but his keen eyes were on the men behind him on foot. His position was now marked. They now had a target.

The black Samurai made himself a difficult target. On both knees in the snow, he faced them, the Swiss submachine gun against his right side. He fired, raking the gun right to left and back again, its deadly chatter tearing into trees, ripping bark, leaves, branches, snow and sending it all flying. And killing two men, the bullets stitching a row of bloody holes across their chests.

They flopped in the snow, and the others ducked. But they fired at him, at the darkness of the tree he now crouched behind. His numbed fingers pulled the hot empty magazine from the smoking gun, while their bullets ripped bark, leaves, snow from his tree, the snow flying in his face and down his back. Snow on his goggles blinded him, and he quickly ripped them off, throwing them away.

He reached in his black canvas bag, pulled out the second magazine, jamming it up into the submachine gun. His eyes searched the wreckage of the three snowmobiles for any sign of life. He saw none, only smoking, hissing machines, ripped apart, overturned and lying on their sides or upside down, dead men trapped underneath or thrown clear and lying bleeding in the snow.

He moved from the tree and out into the moonlight, crouched and running fast over the snow the snowmobiles had just roared across. Then he heard it. One more, this time the same harsh sound but thinner because there was only one machine. But as fast as the black Samurai might be on foot, he had no chance to outrace the machine.

He ran, then started climbing up a small hill, hearing the machine behind him, then turning to see it and suddenly finding himself it its light, the harsh whiteness branding him for impending death. He turned and zig-zagged up the hill, his life depending on the speed and power of his legs. The machine's sound stopped, started, stopped, then started again as it began to take the hill. Bullets kicked up snow near him. The snowmobile's pursuit, its light, were pinpointing him for the remaining men. He wasn't out of rifle range yet.

But he knew one thing, one very important thing. On foot, he could outdistance any man alive, any man. His Samurai training had given him a physical and mental edge, both of which made him a deadly, resourceful enemy. Only the one remaining snowmobile prevented him from outrunning the men who wanted to take his life.

He reached the top of the small hill. The gunfire grew heavier, the noise filling the night air. He dived, rolling down the hill, the cold snow filling his face, covering his body in soft, wet whiteness.

The submachine gun slipped from his hand, disappearing in the snow behind him. His keen ears picked up the sound of the snowmobile now at the top of the hill, slowing down, its driver turning his light left, then right, to pick up the black Samurai.

The light found him. The driver shouted to the men behind him, then gunned the motor, moving swiftly down the hill toward Sand.

Through the haze of snow blinding his eyes, the light sliced through and blinded him more. He was tired, and his lungs burned with fatigue, an ache that made each breath seem as though his chest was filled with needles. He closed his eyes tighter, frantically scooping the snow from them with his left hand, his right hand pulling at his shoulder holster. The raw, ugly sound of the snowmobile grew louder.

The noise seemed to fill his ears, falling on him as though it would swallow him, attacking him like some monster from the dark ages.

His heart pounded, and he fought the panic trying to rise within him and rule him.

He was still blinded. By snow in his eyes, by the light, now brighter and more piercing as the snowmobile bore down on him.

Crablike, he moved to his left, instinctively scrambling away from its sound. He had his Colt .45 ACP Commander clear of his holster when the machine grazed him, sending pain shooting up his right side, knocking him in the air and on his back, the gun flying from his hand and into the snow and darkness.

He refused to give in to the pain. Reaching down into himself, he rolled to his knees, pushing the blackness away from his mind, the blackness that threatened to attack and conquer him from within. He rubbed the back of his right hand across his eyes.

One eye, his right eye, was clear.

The snowmobile driver was having trouble maneuvering the machine around on the uneven snow-covered ground for another run at the black Samurai. The driver fought hard for control and slowly began to complete his U-turn, which would bring him back toward Robert Sand.

Still on his knees, Sand pulled the 22-inch sword from his black canvas bag, clearing it from its scabbard, then rising to his feet, unsteady, pain in his chest but ready to fight like a Samurai.

He held the sword low, behind his leg, out of sight of the driver. His left hand was where it could be seen, empty, high as though in surrender.

The lights hit his face and he crouched, shading his face with his left hand. High on the hill to his left, he heard the sounds of the other attackers. He couldn't see it, but they stopped to watch, each of the men lowering his gun, not wanting to hit the snowmobile driver, but wanting to see the driver power into the black Samurai.

His left side was to the men on the hill, his hand shading his eyes. His right hand, dangling at his side, the short sword pressed flat against his leg, and unseen by anyone in the darkness.

Valbonne's men stood to watch the kill, their eyes on the machine speeding over the snow, heading toward the lone black man standing and waiting to die.

Sand tensed, not with fear, but with concentration.

He would have to make his move almost without seeing the man he must kill to save his own life.

His ears, his eyes, picked up each sensory detail that would help him. He bent his knees. The snowmobile's noise grew louder, and its harsh white light grew brighter and closer.

Three seconds more.

Then, with incredible timing and a skill that had made

him unique even among some of the finest Samurai in Japan's history, Sand made his move.

Quickly, he leaped to his right, barely clear of the snow-mobile, his ears and reflexes timing his movement to clear the machine by only inches. Simultaneously, his sword hand came up and across his body, its razor-sharp blade glinting in the moonlight. With total effort, he stretched his right arm as far as it would go, the blade crossing directly in front of the driver's throat.

Then, with a quick backhand stroke, Sand brought the entire blade across the driver's neck, cutting his throat as he sped by.

The snowmobile sped past the black Samurai, leaving him in darkness.

It raced across the snow, the dead driver slumped over its front, the machine finally crashing loudly into a tree and throwing the blood-covered driver clear and out onto the snow.

The men on the hill were stunned. Unbelievable! They had seen it, and had no choice but to believe it. For brief seconds, none of them moved. Then a flashlight beam cut through the night, picking out the snowmobile, now on its side, still making its ugly raw noise.

The men started down the hill, shouting, cursing loudly.

One of them slipped in the snow, sliding downhill on his behind, his rifle disappearing in the snow. The others paid no attention to him. Their flashlight beams combed the area, the beams seeking, searching.

Quickly, they ran toward the dead man, now lying on his face, his blood seeping out from under him and making a large, red circle for him to lie in.

The men turned from him, their flashlights moving in quick, sporadic patterns through the night, searching out the black man they had just seen kill one of their own.

Around them there was nothing. Only snow and scattered trees, blackness and the cold.

They walked a few steps toward the spot where Sand had leaped to one side while simultaneously slicing the throat of the snowmobile driver.

The black Samurai had disappeared.

CHAPTER 15

Warrior Against Warrior

Valbonne was not yet angry. That could come soon, but not just yet. Now he was uneasy, thinking about the man they had failed to kill tonight. He pressed the white-and-gold antique telephone hard against his ear, feeling it tight on his flesh and bone. His left hand squeezed the receiver. His right hand was clenched tightly in a fist as he spoke slowly, carefully into the telephone.

"He's escaped, disappeared like a handful of black smoke. We had him surrounded, as planned, but he fought his way out of the circle, literally cutting his way out and vanishing."

Salt's flat Arizona voice was cold metal in the Frenchman's ear. "Yeah. He's a hard case, that one. Well, we still got it covered, like we planned. Shit, didn't think his black ass would get out of this one, but what the hell. Time for the next part, huh, Mr. Valbonne?"

"Yes, Mangas. The next part. And Mangas?"

"Yes."

"Don't fail."

"Shit, Mr. Valbonne, I'm sitting right here in Geneva, ready for him. Ain't no way blackie's gonna make it through the night. Right now, he's probably relaxed, you know? Thinks he got it made. Pattin' himself on the back 'cause he sidestepped that little party we set up for him near your place. The dude ain't even thinkin' about walkin' into another hit tonight. See, Mr. Valbonne, that's what's beautiful about it. Not only ain't he expectin' it, I mean his guard is down, but he's walkin' right into it. He's comin' to me."

Valbonne's voice was deliberate, carefully spacing out the words. "Mangas, this man is dangerous."

The Apache was silent. When he did speak, his voice had the feel of sharp steel slicing into a man's throat. "So am I, Mr. Valbonne, so am I."

"I know, Mangas. Man is, after all, the ultimate weapon. He thinks, and that makes him the most deadly killer of all. Call me the moment you complete your business with the black Samurai."

"Yes, Mr. Valbonne."

"No," said Robert Sand.

Zoraida Mahon's voice pleaded through the telephone. "Why can't I see you?"

He sensed her desperation, her fear of suddenly being alone. He knew she felt he was cutting her off, dropping her. That wasn't true. He was trying to save her life. Calmly, his voice sympathetic but firm, he spoke into the receiver. "I had some trouble tonight."

She gasped. "Oh God!"

He winced as pain ripped through his right side. The snowmobile. It had hurt him worse than he had thought. At the time, tension, excitement, cold, took his mind and body off most of the pain. The one-mile run through the snow and darkness had demanded total concentration. Now, back in Geneva and calling from a public telephone booth, he began to feel the cost of tonight in pain.

He had called the Baron in Paris, twice failing to reach him. "Mr. Gray is not in," the Paris switchboard had said. Sand had left messages, giving his third hotel, the Kloten, as the call-back number. Now Zoraida . . .

"I don't have much time," he said to her. "Tonight was a setup, a trap—"

She interrupted, shouting into the telephone. "Who?"

"Zoraida, please don't yell like that. It's like an icepick in my ear. I don't know who. I was expected. They knew I was coming tonight and they were waiting."

"Robert, Robert, please, are you hurt? Just tell me that."

He gritted his teeth against the pain, closing his eyes, both hands clutching the telephone receiver. The pain eased off, backing away. But, like a wolf circling a wounded, dangerous animal, it stayed in sight, ready to strike again.

"I'll be fine. Just *listen*. There's been a leak somewhere,

I don't know where, I don't know who. If I think about it, I'll come up with the answer. I don't even know if I'm being followed, but if I am, I don't want to lead them to you, understand? So stay with Gryff. I'll contact you soon. Whatever you do, don't go outside, and above all, don't come looking for me. You could get killed."

"Robert, I—"

"Goodbye, Zoraida." He hung up. Leaning against the telephone booth, he wiped perspiration from his forehead with the back of his right hand. He breathed deeply, then slid the door open and stepped out into the cold night.

The Apache, red headband across his forehead, white paint under his eyes and across the bridge of his long, flat nose, stood still in the darkness, his keen ears listening.

He was in Robert Sand's suite at the Kloten Hotel.

Pale-yellow moonlight came through windows on two sides of the luxury suite. For Salt, moonlight was enough to see by. He was bare-chested, tan buckskin leggings wrapped tightly around him from waist to calves, hand-made blue-and-white beaded moccasins on his feet. War dress. Only worn when he attacked alone and at night.

The cunning Apache had not lied to Valbonne. When it came to killing, the Apache was an excellent thinker. From the names of Sand's three hotels and aliases, the Indian had made a decision. The trap near Valbonne's chateau would be handled by men he selected from Valbonne's guards. A back-up ambush, this one handled by Salt personally—and alone—would be set up at the black man's hotel.

Salt had figured out the hotel Sand would choose out of the three. The Hotel Waage was eliminated. That was the scene of the fight with Saraga's men and the rescue of the woman. This black Samurai wouldn't go back there again.

A check of the second hotel showed he had stayed there last night, under one of the aliases Salt had listed for him.

That left only one hotel, the Kloten, the one place the black hadn't yet appeared in. The room had been kept ready, and it had been easy to find out that it hadn't been occupied by anyone in almost a week. The Kloten. That's where the killer Apache waited.

The Kloten, on Kramgasse, was small, quiet, expensive. It was twelve stories high, an old hotel, with an easily accessible roof. From the roof, Salt had lowered himself down to the ninth floor, dangling from a rope, his right hand gripping a knife. Swiftly, quietly, he pried open a window.

Seconds later, he stood inside on the highly polished brown wooden floor, hearing sounds of footsteps walking along the hallway in front of the suite and men speaking in French.

A murderous-looking ax, its gleaming blade honed to a killing edge earlier that day by Salt, was shoved in his silver-studded rawhide belt.

What he held in his left hand, however, was the most deadly weapon of all. It was a black carrying case used for small animals. It had hung from his left shoulder when he climbed off the roof and down along the rope.

Now he held it up in the moonlight and darkness, his eyes staring at the airholes in the front and the wire-covered openings on either side. A corner of his mouth turned up and he walked slowly toward the bathroom, careful to touch nothing, to bump into nothing. Up on the roof, he had walked barefoot in snow, his moccasins tucked in his belt. Only when he was ready to climb down the rope, did he sit on the edge of the roof and put on the moccasins.

He would leave no wet footprints on the shiny brown wooden floor. This black Samurai, Salt admitted, was a warrior, and Apaches respected warriors. The Indian had given his respect grudgingly to the black man, because tonight he had earned it. Tonight, however, the black man could take that respect with him to his grave.

He found the bathroom, huge fingers fumbling until they reached the light switch, his hard eyes squinting when the harsh, bright light came on. Salt blinked quickly, again and again, and even while his eyes accustomed themselves to the light, he began doing what he was there for.

His eyes looked at the thick, white-painted wood of the door and he closed it, bending low and running his fingers along the bottom. Between the door and the black-and-white tile floor there was an almost unnoticeable crack. However, the Apache wanted to be sure.

Reaching into his waistband, he took out a roll of black tape and tore off a two-foot strip. He stuck the strip to the bottom of the door, as if to make it airtight, and when he finished, he spun around to the black carrying case sitting on the floor behind. He thumbed open the two silver locks, but he didn't open the case. Not just yet.

His wide, cruel mouth was unsmiling and his face was tense as his right hand took out the knife tucked into his tan leggings along his calf. Beads of sweat popped out on his brown forehead as he poked at the top of the case with the blade, suddenly flipping it open, then standing up and moving back away from it.

The cunning Apache knew how important heat was now. Up on the roof, in the snow and darkness, it had been cold. Here in the bathroom, it was warm.

The rattlesnake slid silently out of the black carrying case, in search of warmth.

Slowly it went over the side of the case, then eased along the black-and-white tile floor, its thin black-and-orange body bunching up, then stretching out, as it searched for heat. It hissed and its tail rattles made a harsh, dry sound, chilling to hear. It moved away from the Apache, its flat head gray and ugly, its eyes high on the outside of its head and bright as new small black buttons. The head quickly darted left and right, forked red tongue flicking out between dripping needle-sharp fangs, then disappearing back into the rattlesnake's pale-white jaws. Salt picked up the carrying case.

Sneering, his eyes on the deadly snake, the Apache reached behind him for the light switch, flicked it off, and quickly stepped out of the room, closing the door quietly and tightly.

Minutes later, he stood on the roof, neither his mind nor his body reacting to the bitter cold. He looked over the roof down toward the window he had just climbed through. He was waiting for a light to go on, and minutes after it did, he would climb down the rope again, slip through the window, and watch a black man die.

The black Samurai leaned against the door, his eyes narrowed with caution as his gaze swept his hotel suite with one quick, complete glance. Nothing had been touched, nothing seemed out of place, and there were no marks on the polished brown wooden floor.

Robert Sand sensed no one in the room, and yet . . .

His Samurai training had taught him to think swiftly, and above all, to react swiftly. Samurai training meant recognizing crisis and danger, then reacting to them. Above all, never, never dismissing a warning, no matter how slight.

Death had reached out for him tonight, then passed him by. Could death still be near? Was it going to try again so soon?

His right hand gripped his short sword, the blade brown with the dried blood of the man he had killed tonight. He carried it low as he walked throughout the suite, finding no one as he walked into the bedrooms, checked closets, then back to the living room. No one. Nothing. Perhaps he was still excited, tensed and keyed-up after his narrow escape tonight. Perhaps.

He winced, his face knotting at the pain in his right side where the snowmobile had grazed him. A hot bath. That's what he needed. In seconds, his black leather coat and turtleneck sweater were tossed across a chair, and bare-chested, he headed toward the bathroom. First he'd run the water, clean his sword, maybe try the Baron one more time. After that, he'd sit in the tub for a while.

He rubbed the back of his neck with his left hand, the sword still hanging down in his right hand. Master Konuma. He smiled, thinking of his old master and how he had never varied in his rules of training. Running. Always running, every day, even when only training a half day. Legs. That was the key. Legs. Tonight, his life had been saved because of Master Konuma's tough, un-bending rules.

The black Samurai opened the bathroom door, switched on the light, and again tensed with the pain, stopping to stroke his right side with his left hand. He closed his eyes in fatigue and agony, then half-opened them, bending over the bathtub to turn on the water.

He reached out for the hot-water tap with his left hand, and—

In less than two seconds, it happened. Quick and deadly.

A hissing sound, swiftly followed by the harsh, dry rattling noise and a death strike almost faster than the eye could see. He heard the sounds—the hiss, the rattle—and he opened his eyes. But pain and fatigue and a slight relaxing of his caution had made him a fraction slower than he might have been.

The snake's flat, hideous head snapped forward like a whip, its fangs digging into Sand's left forearm, the needles of pain tearing into his flesh and moving swiftly into his body. He fought the panic inside him that threatened to paralyze him with fear.

Dropping to his knees on the hard, cool tile floor, he brought his sword hand up high, then down in a savage backhand stroke, severing the snake's head from its body, the warm blood spurting up on Sand's bare chest. The hideous headless body twisted and slithered along the white enamel bathtub, its frightening movements leaving a trail of red blood on the bottom of the tub.

"Too late, Samurai!"

Sand, his brown forehead beaded with perspiration, his heart beating fast, snapped his head to his left. The huge, bare-chested Apache stood in the bathroom doorway, his muscular legs wide apart, one hand fingering the keen blade of the small ax stuck in his waistband. His eyes were cruel and bright with triumph and he allowed himself a small smile.

The black Samurai was determined not to die on his knees.

In a microcosm of a second, his keen mind told him that he must move quickly, with as perfect technique as possible. His own life was now measured in minutes. Perhaps less. He had trained to face death. He knew what a Samurai must do.

Still on his knees, he turned swiftly, his back to the Apache. Rising to a crouch, he back-kicked hard, driving his right foot into Salt's stomach, the strong kick pushing the Indian back into the living room. Salt's arms flailed wildly as he tried to keep his balance, but he went back, back, back until he landed, half-sitting, half-lying, on the floor.

Sand had bought himself precious seconds.

Placing the sword's cutting edge directly on the snake bite, he gritted his teeth and sliced into his own flesh, once, twice, making a bloody X over the two tiny holes. Keeping his eyes on the huge Apache as he staggered backward and fell, the black Samurai sucked at the wound, drawing deep, filling his mouth with his own blood, then spitting it out. He did it again, filling his mouth with the warm, salt taste, then spitting it out on the tile floor.

His mouth was filled with blood for a third time when the Apache scrambled to his feet, jerked the ax from his silver-studded rawhide belt, then charged the black Samurai.

The Apache yelled. "Aieeeee!"—a horrifying, blood-chilling sound.

For the third time, Sand spit out the mouthful of his own blood, gripping the small sword tightly in his right hand. He made no move to leave the bathroom, his quick mind turning the small space to his advantage. As he had figured, Salt changed speed slightly, to allow his six-foot-five frame to come through the door. It took a keen eye to see that he had changed rhythm and slightly altered his body position, but Sand's eye was keen.

Salt held the ax high, then brought it down hard at Sand's head. "The sword is magic in your hands." Sand had been told this by Master Konuma. Night after night, when the other Samurai slept, Robert Sand had snuck into the dojo, where by moonlight he had practiced the long sword and the short sword until his arms ached and his eyes burned with the salt of his own perspiration.

Tonight, once again, his training would have to stand between him and death.

He lifted the sword high and above his forehead, catching the ax at its handle, and without a second's hesitation, brought the blade across Salt's bare chest, a stroke that was done so quickly that it had been entirely completed almost a full two seconds before the blood began to appear, first in bright red beads, then in larger amounts.

The cut was painful, but it was far from killing. It would take more than that to stop the Apache.

Salt's eyes went wide, but he gave no other sign that he was hurt. His leg kicked at Sand, catching the black Samurai in his chest, knocking him off his feet and backward toward the tub.

The breath went out of Sand, and he winced as his right side crashed into the tub. With the ease of thousands of practice sessions, he tossed the small sword from his right hand to his left, catching the oncoming Apache unawares. Sand's counterattack was low. He was almost flat on his back and there was no other way.

Swiftly, he backhanded the blade across Salt's ankles, slicing through the leggings. The Apache inhaled loudly, moving backward, crouching, his cruel dark eyes focused on the black man, but now his eyes held a new caution and respect. A thin line of blood crept through the left legging, but like the chest cut, it was more painful than paralyzing.

The Apache had painfully learned the small space was not to his advantage. He backed up slowly, never taking his eyes from Sand, the ax blade gleaming brightly in the living-room lights.

Sand moved forward to meet him, his mind crowding out the pain in his side, his left arm bloody where he had sliced it, his mouth and chin now red with his own blood as well.

Salt faked. He darted in, stopped, stepped to the side, then backhanded the ax toward Sand's head. Any other man would have been dead, and the black Samurai didn't miss death by much. He turned with Salt's movements, at the last possible second blocking the ax blade with his sword.

A table overturned, crashing to the floor with a small bowl of freshly cut red and white flowers, the water turning the tan carpet black.

Warrior against warrior.

Salt pressed hard, pushing his ax down hard against Sand's small sword. Blackness clawed at Sand, and he felt as though his head was wrapped in ice. He was in pain, and he was tired, and there was the poison, the snake venom. How much was still in him? How much longer did he have to live?

He yielded, slowly, grudgingly, inch by inch, letting the Apache push him backward and down toward the floor. Their faces were only inches apart—the Apache, flat-featured, white paint under his eyes and across his nose making him frightening to look at, his eyes bright with determined hate, his face wet with sweat; Sand, his perspiring face grim and intense with the drive to survive, knowing his life was on the line and that every second was against him.

The black Samurai's move was sudden. Quickly he fell backward and to the tan rug, his left hand reaching out for the Apache's wrist, pulling him down too. As Sand went backward, his right foot came up hard against the

Indian's stomach. Now Sand's back was on the rug, his right foot in Salt's stomach.

Pulling down hard with his hands, and pushing up hard with his right foot, he threw the Indian in tomoenage, the circle throw, one of the most spectacular techniques in judo. The Apache flew overhead, turning once in the air, knocking a table and a lamp loudly to the floor, crashing loudly to the floor himself, his muscular body thumping against the carpet.

Sand rolled over, turning to look at Salt. The Apache was on his hands and knees, shaking his head left to right to clear it, his bare chest heaving with exhaustion and hurt. As the black Samurai fumbled for his sword just inches from his hand, he felt iron claws of pain clutch at his chest, and he moaned once, his eyes wide. He breathed deeply, desperate to draw air into himself.

Salt staggered to his feet, groggy but still dangerous, his eyes moving quickly from the black Samurai, then across the floor. The ax. It lay on the tan rug, the sharp steel gleaming with diamond brilliance. He staggered toward it.

Sand breathed deeply, slowly. He was on his knees, the short sword clenched in his hand.

The darkness that he had pushed back for the past few minutes now crowded in on him again, and he grew dizzy. As if in a dream, he heard noises, voices, and a thumping against the door.

The sword slipped from his fingers, and his mouth was open as he looked at the Apache bending over to pick up his ax. As Salt's huge fingers curled around the handle, his bright eyes gleamed. He turned toward Sand.

The black Samurai, kneeling on the floor, bleeding and rapidly sinking into unconsciousness, perhaps death, used his one remaining weapon, his Samurai spirit. With agonizingly slow movements, he faced the Apache and yelled, "Kiaiiii!" His shout filled the room. If he had to die, it would be as a Samurai and not on his knees.

The Apache stopped, his eyes wide in surprise.

Sand pressed his hands against the floor, his eyes now slits, his face wet with perspiration and his own blood. He struggled to his feet. Samurai. Again he yelled—"Kiaaaiiiiii!"

He was on his feet. Salt was moving closer to him.

Darkness triumphed. It reached out with a swift, savage motion and swallowed the black Samurai.

CHAPTER 16

Survival

Valbonne hung up, his hand still gripping the telephone receiver, his mouth in a small, tight grin of satisfaction. He turned to look at Salt. "The police tell me the black Samurai's brother arrives from America sometime this afternoon to claim the body and take it back to America. You've done well, Mangas."

The Apache looked down at the white bandages wrapped across his bare chest. The right leg of his faded blue jeans had been slit up from the bottom to the knee, showing the bandage wrapped around his calf. His eyes met Valbonne's. "Tell you something, Mr. Valbonne. He was a ball buster, this guy. Damn snake bit him, and man, I'm telling you, he didn't panic or come apart like just about anyone else would. Out in Arizona, I seen some tough people, but ain't one of them that didn't fold up when a snake got 'em or even came near 'em. Not this guy. He fought back hard, like nothing had happened to him. Know somethin', Mr. Valbonne? For a minute back there when I was fightin' him, I kinda got a strange feelin', almost like me and him, well, like we was brothers. Bet it sounds strange to you, huh?"

Valbonne nodded. He understood. "In one sense, you were brothers, Mangas. You both were warriors, and you both fought as well as you could. Except that you won."

"Yeah, sure. You know, when they started to break down his hotel door, I had to cut out. But, well, it's like the old days. You fought against a brave man and even after you killed him, you respected him. Back in that room, I wanted to stay there a little while, maybe just look at him or somethin'—oh hell, I don't know. He's the only one so far who fought back. No one else did. Black Samurai. Hell, he'd make a fuckin' good black Apache. Damn sure would."

Smiling, Valbonne pointed to the bandages around Salt's chest. "Guess he left a mark on you in more ways than one."

Salt's mouth moved in a wry half-grin. "Yeah. Guess so. Startin' to hurt and itch, too. Guess the stitches are dryin'. I can still get around, though. Anythin' else you got for me?"

Valbonne pursed his lips, looked down at the floor, then at the huge Apache. "As a matter of fact, Mangas, I do. For one thing, we know that the late black Samurai had at least one other man working with him, a Mr. Gray in Paris. So far, my contacts there have been unable to learn anything about any Mr. Gray, which seems odd in itself. There's no way of knowing any more about Mr. Gray or our black friend, at least from Mr. Perrin, anyway."

Salt chuckled, the small noise rumbling deep within his chest.

"Perrin's walkin' around on the bottom of Lake Geneva. I dumped him so far out there that they ain't gonna find his ass even on judgment day."

"That's our next problem, in a sense—people who talk. Our scientific help have outdone themselves. It looks as though they will have the bomb in working order sometime tonight, tomorrow morning at the latest."

"Hey, that's great, Mr. Valbonne. Really great. Guess driving them people day and night paid off."

Valbonne smiled with smug pride. "Yes. Perhaps we have our black friend to thank for that. He forced us all to press harder, and the results have been pleasing. It means we're that much closer to the remaining $50 million final payment. It means we can move the bomb out tomorrow, and that's exactly what I plan to do. Move it out tomorrow, with a change in departure port and the landing port as well. If Mr. Gray or anyone else is aware of our timetable, well, their information, as the Americans would say, is inoperative. No good."

Salt nodded his head. He understood. "I guess that means we won't be needin' them people any more."

Valbonne nodded his head once, smiling. "Bravo, my

Apache friend. Indeed we won't. And so we kill them, with the exception of Berk. He's been making reports to Saraga about the bomb's progress. But our Japanese friend is not so revenge-minded that he'll hand over $50 million without first hearing from someone he trusts that the bomb is in good working order."

"That's what Berk's gonna do, huh?"

"If he wants to enjoy a few more hours of living, yes, Mangas, that's what he'll do. I suggest that when we dispose of the other scientists that Mr. Berk not be around. It might upset him. He, naturally, will be present when Saraga appears. Saraga will be there at the final payoff. He won't turn over the money until the bomb's in Canada and Berk assures him the bomb is functional. That's the last we'll see of Mr. Berk. He'll be taken to New York to connect the bomb to the trigger and I doubt if he'll live much longer after that."

Salt nodded in agreement.

Valbonne continued. "Interesting that our little bomb is so much smaller yet twice as powerful as the two used in Japan 29 years ago. Think of 40,000 tons of TNT exploding in the center of that overcrowded American metropolis. That's our bomb, Mangas. And it's due to go off directly under the Empire State Building."

"I was in New York once—did I tell you, Mr. Valbonne? I always thought that if that town ever got bombed, with all those glass buildings around? Well, it would be like a million knives flyin' through the air, all that glass, you know?"

"Graphically put, Mangas. Yes, it will be something to see, provided you're looking at it in a newspaper. Anyway, our bomb is compact, smaller and convenient for shipping. It can be dismantled, taken anywhere, reassembled, and then used. Above all, it has the benefit of new knowledge, and it is extremely deadly. All we need is a few more hours, then it's almost over. If we get visitors at that point, there'll be no problem, because there'll be nothing for them to see here."

"The scientists?"

"Oh yes. As I was saying, they become useless the moment they finish. And they can be traced to us. So, sometime tomorrow, we drink a toast, all of us, them, you, me. We all drink one of my most outstanding liquors, and for this I think I'll use the Napoleon brandy, the 174-year-old bottle."

Salt chuckled. "Blow the dust off mine first."

Valbonne smiled. "Don't worry about the brandy, Mangas. Drink up, enjoy it. The brandy will be excellent, I'm sure. But the glasses, now that will be a different matter."

"Don't understand you, Mr. Valbonne."

"Simple, my Apache friend. It's all very simple. There'll be no suspicion as I uncork the bottle in front of them, and we all drink from it, me included. But the men will still die, and they'll die from drinking. Their glasses will be coated with an unseen substance I am assured is fatal and leaves no trace. A Russian sold this poison to me, and I'm told it's all the rage in Moscow these days, when certain people wish to dispose of other people and not cause a disturbance while doing so."

"Smart. Real smart. We dump 'em in the lake, too?"

"Yes, Mangas, we dump them in Lake Geneva as well. Mr. Perrin undoubtedly will welcome the company. Tomorrow, we can also toast the memory of your fellow warrior, the black Samurai—that is, if you'd like."

Salt was silent. Then he said softly, "Yeah, sure. He had some pair of balls. Yeah, why not."

The Baron said, "You look cute wrapped in white. Y'all oughta wear it more often."

Robert Sand opened his eyes, then closed them tightly as the pain flashed through his head, turning everything around him a fuzzy red. He opened his eyes again wider, trying to focus on William Baron Clarke, who sat in a wide-armed brown leather chair.

Sand was lying in bed in a room he had never seen before.

"Lemme answer some of your questions," said the Baron. "Then you can answer some of mine. OK, well, let's see. After Perrin squeezed them hotels and your names outta me, I got on the panicky side. Far as I was concerned, the shit had hit the fan ten times over. I felt bad about it and wouldn't have done it if he hadn't said the bomb was movin' out soon, earlier than we figured. Damn, son, you gotta know that seven million people fixin' to get blowed up is a goddam hard thing to live with. So I told him. I couldn't reach you myself, seein' as how you was out frolickin' across the snow-covered countryside and all. Left messages for you, but it seems that Valbonne's men picked them up instead. They knew to look for 'Mr. Gray.' And when you was callin' *me*, I was on my way to Geneva, looks like."

Sand sat up in bed. Zoraida walked into the room, looked at him, and ran toward the bed. "Robert, oh Robert!"

Her hands touched her cheeks, and she seemed glad to see him awake and alive. "God, I've worried about you, really I have."

"Young lady," said the Baron in a loud Texas drawl, "get your pretty ass outta here until we're finished, and shut the door behind you, goodbye!"

She heard him, but it didn't bother her. She backed out of the room, her eyes on Sand, her pretty face and green eyes smiling at him.

Sand and the former President of the United States were alone again.

"As I was saying before that good-lookin' piece walked in, I came here to get on top of things, to check out Perrin, and to see, well, to make sure you was all right. I checked with Mr. Gryff, who, by the way, owns this here fancy country house we are all in at the moment. He hadn't heard from you, but the little lady had. We knew you were in Geneva. Findin' you wasn't hard after that, and it seems we found you just in time. By the way, you yell loud as hell. Musta scared the Indian outta his moccasins."

Sand said, "I'm thirsty. Yes, I think it helped."

"Water over there, yeah, right there. Help yourself. Anyway, when we get to the Kloten, we hear this racket goin' on inside your place. You colored folks sure like to carry on at night, don't you? Anyway, we hollered, me and Frank Pines, he's with me, and Mr. Gryff. We started John Wayne-ing the door, and I guess the noise scared off whoever was ready to snuff out your candle."

Sand was quiet. Then he said, "Salt. The Apache. Last thing I remembered was him walking toward me with an ax in his hand. Guess I passed out. He probably thought I was dead."

"Ain't no surprise. That rattler what bit you wasn't just whistlin' 'Dixie.' Did you bleed yourself?"

"As quickly as I could. The Apache kept me busy, and

I never got to finish the job." He looked at his bandaged left forearm.

"Damn snake almost finished you. We saw the ugly bastard, sliced up in the bathroom. Ain't nothin' like what we got down home. In Texas, one that size ain't no more than a cockroach."

"It almost got the job done."

The Baron chuckled. " 'Almost' *never* got no job done. Yeah, that bite had you down, but you ain't out. Not by a long shot. I took out more blood myself, right in the room, and we had you taken to the morgue."

Sand frowned. "Rushing things, weren't you?"

The Baron looked smug. "You ain't a politician, sonny. I am, one of the best that ever drew breath. A doctor was in the ambulance workin' on you, a doctor of my acquaintance, I might add."

"Perrin?"

"No. After what happened to you, I'm sure Perrin's dead as button shoes. No, I got another sawbones, and when you came out of that ambulance, you was covered up with a white sheet. Now ain't that a caution? Black man under a white sheet." The Baron laughed and slapped his knee.

Sand said, "When you stop rolling over the floor, maybe you'll tell me—"

"Sorry, son, can't resist levity sometimes. Anyway, took you inside the morgue, had you pronounced dead, had your 'brother'—that is to say, a black Secret Service agent now guardin' my Presidential body—come from Paris and claim your corpus delicti. That's why you're here. Your brother and a coffin flew back to America, for the benefit of curious and interested parties."

"Hungry," said Sand.

The Baron roared, "Gryff, git him some food, some real food, none of that foreign stuff, you hear? Meat, some goddam meat. Now!"

Sand stretched his arms wide, crossed them, then stretched them overhead. "How many hours have I been out?"

The Baron chuckled. "Hours? Son, you almost did die for real. We jabbed you with more needles than you ever wanna hear about. You been out almost two days."

The black Samurai was stunned. "Two days! You're kidding!"

"No way. You been tossin', turnin', sweatin', moanin'. You ain't all that much fun to be around when you're dying, lemme tell you."

"Valbonne, the bomb, what—"

"Hey, whoa, ease up. First thing was to keep you alive. Yeah, we on top of the bomb, don't sweat it. Expectin' a call any minute now, and—"

There was a knock on the door. The Baron said, "Yeah?"

It opened and Mr. Gryff stood there, smiling politely and coldly, but obviously awed by the presence of the tall Texan who had ruled one of the most powerful nations in the history of the world. Power. The German understood that. "Telephone, Herr—I mean Mr.—President."

The Baron said, "Thank you, Gryff," in a loud voice that meant "Get the hell out of here." He added, "Tell Frank Pines to listen in downstairs. I'll take it up here."

Mr. Gryff bowed, and looked as though he wanted to click his heels and say *"Heil,"* but he did neither. He shut the door and the Baron got up, walked to the telephone, and picked up the receiver. Seconds later, he said, "Frank? OK, go ahead."

He listened intently, eyes sparkling brightly at again playing the game of power, destiny and danger. Retirement wasn't for him. It never would be.

He let out a deep breath, then said, "Fine. Come on back as quick as you can." He hung up, turning to Sand. "Got some Swiss police friends of Gryff's to go with two of my men. Went out to Valbonne's chateau and to that little old valley you told me about. Couldn't figure out what else to do, and frankly, son, for a while there, it looked like you might not make it. Anyway, Valbonne's gone. Worse, the valley's empty. So's the ski lodge."

"Empty?" Sand was puzzled. "How could that be?"

"Don't know. Perrin was obviously lyin', we know that now. He was settin' you up for a hit, so he was lying' to me about the bomb bein' ready. All I can figure out is that maybe they *did* get it ready and moved out, or they think we're closin' in and they've gone somewhere else. I don't know what the hell to do now, damn it. If that bomb's undercover, if they've hidden it someplace else, we gonna have the devil's own time findin' it."

Sand's face was tense, his eyes narrowed in thought. He stared straight ahead, concentrating, then he said, "Get on the phone quickly. Call Ganai in Tokyo. Find out if Saraga's ships have gone anywhere special in the past few hours. If so, where. Find out anything you can about his ships. Where they are is where the bomb is. Check if any of his ships are heading to North America. Also, get a helicopter in the air. Check roads leading toward Germany, the south of France and the west coast of France. See if any trucks are on the road that might have come from here. Do you have people who could check these ports?"

The Baron's grin was sly, smug. Locking both hands behind his neck, he drawled, "Son, I was the best in the world at what I did. Politickin', some folks called it. Power-crazy is another term I heard a lot of. But one thing I'm proud of: nobody ever called me dumb. Now those questions you just asked me, I been askin' other people beginning with when it looked like you was goin' to die and endin' with five minutes ago. Those orders you gave me, I already gave a lot of other people. The questions are out, the answers ain't come in yet. But they will. They goddam well better. So relax, lean back on your bed of pain, and allow me to show you how I got to be the all-knowin' son of a bitch I am."

Four hours later, the Baron said in a voice hoarse from almost constant talking, "Bottom line now. Saraga's got twenty ships out on the water now, goin' everywhere you can name. Six are headin' to North America—New Orleans, Galveston, Vancouver. Most interestin' one of all is the *Yokohama Princess*. She's bound for Toronto, onliest one he's got headin' toward the East Coast."

Sand said, "You're sure about that?"

"I made sure. Ain't nothin' else belongin' to Saraga coming near the East Coast for two weeks more. I think the *Princess* is what we're after."

"Where did it sail from?"

"Japan to Cherbourg, France, bound for Toronto. Can't get any more plainer'n that. No sense in them takin' a plane if they still got to hook it up to the trigger. If Berk's with them, he's got five days for any last-minute work before landin'. Saraga's left Tokyo, no word on where he's headin', and Valbonne's disappeared, too."

"They'll both turn up in Toronto. That's where the final payment, the $50,000,000, will be turned over."

The Baron sipped from a cup of lukewarm black coffee

and made a face. "I can put a plane up in the air and comb the Atlantic till I find them bastards. They'll be dead and drowned in less than a day."

"No."

"No? Did I hear you say no? You must still be sick."

"Saraga's using normal shipping lanes. Bomb the *Yokohama Princess* and if that atomic bomb goes off, you could be destroying nearby ships or starting a tidal wave that could overturn those ships. Passenger or military, it doesn't matter. Someone will die, and there might even be trouble if it's a ship belonging to a nation bent on making trouble."

The Baron rubbed his unshaven jaw, his huge hand brushing uncut black-and-gray stubble. "Damn! Must be gettin' old, I guess. Sounds like something that idiot now sitting in the White House just might do."

Sand grinned. "Forget him, everybody else is trying like hell to. About the ship, let it land. We'll be in Toronto to meet it. That's where the money will be turned over, that's where Saraga's got to show. The money won't be released without his personal OK, and he'll want to be there when the bomb's loaded on trucks and brought into New York."

"Good thinkin'. Damn Canadian border. It's like a sieve. You could bring a herd of purple elephants across it, and nobody would even ask you how many or what color."

"That's what Saraga figures. I'll need some of your men, Frank Pines especially."

"You got 'em. Eight at least. Some will be with the missus. She's in Paris. Lovely little lady. She's used to my gallopin' off by now."

Sand walked across the room slowly, then back again.

"Feelin' OK, son?"

"I feel like a man who's just been hit by a rattlesnake and almost killed by an Apache Indian."

The Baron chuckled. "Son, you just been baptized. I think you 'bout ready now to go into politics. Well, let's go travelin'."

CHAPTER 17

Payoff

Toronto.

Gozo Saraga sat in the back seat of the limousine, pearl-gray overcoat around his shoulders, dark-blue hat on his lap. His gray gloves lay on top of the hat, and his left hand brushed imaginary dust from his immaculate, expensive gray suit. He looked out of the window at the darkness around him, then turned to Valbonne, sitting on his right. "Mr. Berk assures me the merchandise is functional. All that remains is the final coupling. Bomb to trigger. This time device—it is something new?"

Valbonne smiled. "Yes. In essence this bomb, though smaller, is far superior to the one used at both Hiroshima and Nagasaki. There have been advancements in 29 years —atomic energy, explosives, radar, electronics. All of these things combined have given us an excellent weapon. I think you will be pleased."

Saraga nodded. "The scientists who worked on this project, are they—"

"Dead? Yes. Five days ago, before we left Europe. We drank a toast, which for all except Mr. Berk turned out to be a farewell toast. When we conclude our business here tonight, I and my associate, the Apache Indian you met tonight, will return to Europe. There are several people in England, France and Switzerland who I feel should be eliminated to prevent them from connecting us with the bomb."

Saraga nodded. "I leave that in your hands. The girl, Miss Mahon?"

"My men are looking for her now. Geneva, Zurich, I've even got people looking for her in other cities. So far, there's no trace of her. If I find her, what shall I do?"

Saraga looked at him, then turned away to stare out into the darkness at the ship docked nearby. It was his ship, the *Yokohama Princess*, and it had sailed from Cherbourg, France, five days ago, carrying the atomic bomb built by Valbonne and $50 million in American dollars, German marks, Swiss francs. Saraga's silence meant, "Kill the woman when you find her."

Valbonne understood. He was in Toronto to collect the $50 million. He had brought Salt with him, along with four other men from Europe and four men he had hired here. All were armed with automatic weapons and handguns.

Saraga had his ship's crew, sullen, silent men who spoke no English and obeyed his every command. "I will give the signal to unload the money," said Saraga. He tapped the glass partition in front of him three times and the driver honked his horn twice. "When you have satisfied yourself that it is all there, I shall take Mr. Berk off your hands and be on my way. After he has completed his work in New York for me, I shall no longer have need of his services."

Valbonne shrugged. "Suit yourself. Where will you be when the bomb goes off?"

"I thought perhaps right here. I will oversee the project in New York myself. I'm sure you have no wish to accompany me. Once the bomb is in position, and the timer set, I shall leave and return here. An excellent vantage point, don't you think?"

"Personally, I prefer something more distant myself, like Europe. We'll be returning there tomorrow." Valbonne looked at his watch, then toward the *Yokohama Princess*. Saraga's men were beginning to unload the bomb, huge cranes lifting heavy crates out of the ship's hold and swinging them over the side and down to the dock, setting the crates on long, flat trucks.

Valbonne would dispose of the $50 million here in Toronto, receiving other currency and gold bullion which he would then ship to Switzerland through legitimate channels, under a false name. But first, he would count the money, every penny of it, all $50 million. He and the Apache. Salt towered over the smaller Japanese, and they regarded him as a man to handle carefully. The ship's captain and first mate spoke English enough to be understood. They knew he was onboard to see the money carried off. And without a word being said, they knew Salt would be trouble if the money wasn't all there.

It was.

"Put the money in that warehouse," he said to the captain, pointing it out to him. The warehouse had been rented days before the ship landed, and only Valbonne's men had been near it during that time. "We'll count it inside." Salt didn't say what would happen if the money wasn't all there. He didn't have to.

Saraga's voice hissed at Valbonne, and both of the men felt the tension in the back seat of the limousine. "Who are they, who are they?" The Japanese's right hand gripped the small Frenchman's wrist, making him frown with pain. He pulled his hand away from the Japanese but kept his eyes on the four uniformed men, now tying up a Canadian police boat to the pier and turning to walk toward the limousine.

Each of the men wore a dark-green uniform, black cap and holstered pistol. Two carried flashlights, one a clipboard, and one carried a hand radio.

When they reached the limousine, Valbonne rolled down the window and smiled. "Yes, officer?"

"You in charge, sir?" The speaker was a tall, blond-haired young man with calm blue eyes and an easy smile. He was very polite.

"Yes, officer, what can we do for you? Frankly, we weren't expecting anyone here tonight." Valbonne spoke slowly, distinctly, his shrewd senses acute and alert. The tall, polite young man didn't seem to notice that some of the men on the darkened pier had stopped what they were doing and were staring at him. Three or four of the men were moving casually toward the uniformed men and the limousine.

The tall young man smiled. "Tell you the truth, sir, we didn't expect to be here, but, well, what can you do. You get a tip and you check it out, especially when it involves a guy who just can't stop setting fires."

"Fires?" Valbonne smiled, relaxing, leaning back against the expensive mink seat covers. He turned to look at Saraga, still grim, but with a face relaxing by inches.

"Yes, sir," said the polite young man. "He's burned up quite a few million dollars in property, timber and public buildings. Loves to play with matches. Unfortunately, a fire up here can do a lot of damage and it's no joke. We lose millions of dollars in timber every year, and that's more than just pulp for paper. It's a lot of jobs."

Valbonne gave a small smile, shrugging his shoulders as if to say life is hard, friend. "So he's around here?"

"Well, sir, that's a tip we'd like to check out, if it wouldn't be too much trouble. Frankly, he doesn't like to work near people, like say what you've got around here. He likes quiet, does his work mostly at night. I'm pretty sure, for instance, that he couldn't have gotten on that ship with the crew on it."

Valbonne nodded, always smiling, handling the situation calmly. From out of the darkness, Salt appeared as if by magic. The Frenchman called to him and the four uniformed men turned quickly to look at the huge Apache. "It's all right, Mangas, these gentlemen are looking for someone, a criminal of some sort."

Turning back to Valbonne, the polite young man said, "Sir, we've already radioed that we've stopped here, but from the looks of it, we don't have anything really to do. I mean there's just too many people around here for our friend to consider doing anything. But just to make sure, may I speak with the captain and first mate of the ship? If they give me the all-clear, if they tell me nobody's been on board except who should be there, that'll be good enough for my report."

Valbonne turned to Saraga as if to say, fool, there's no problem. Kill them and whoever is on the other end of the radio could be here in minutes. Out loud, he said to the young man, "Send one of your men over to the ship and ask for Captain Ohara and Mr. Kuriya. That's his first mate. Both speak some English. I'm sure you'll find that they have nothing to report regarding visitors."

Unseen in the darkness, Valbonne's hand pressed down hard on Saraga's thigh, motioning him to stay back in the car and out of sight. The Japanese shipping magnate was world-famous. It wouldn't do for him to be seen where he was not expected.

As for Valbonne, his face was half-hidden by darkness. Soon this minor interruption would be over. He raised his voice. "Mangas, you may go back inside the warehouse now. Everyone else, go about his business. Officer, my men have been in the warehouse for over and hour and I can assure you that there's no one else on the premises."

The young man smiled. "Sir, as I told you, we want to make it home tonight as soon as we can. We're all hockey fans, you know, so it's fine with us if you say things are quiet around here. Just one thing, though. Those four trucks there—"

Valbonne stiffened, his jaw tensing. Saraga's intake of breath could be almost heard from where he sat hidden in darkness. His muscular Japanese chauffeur reached inside his black jacket for the .357 Magnum he carried.

"Like I was saying, sir, those trucks. Sure would make my job easier if you would have your drivers move them off the pier, say down toward the end there and out of sight, maybe a few yards to the left. Just want to make sure that there's as few hiding places for our boy as possible. If he's determined to fire up this pier, I want to make it hard for him, understand. Give him no place to hide." The young man smiled, his white teeth even, spotless.

Valbonne took a deep breath, looked at Saraga, then let out the air. Both men were silent, letting the tension slide from them. Finally, the Frenchman turned to the young officer, forced a smile, licked his lips, and spoke slowly. "Sounds fair enough to me, officer. We'll do just that. OK if we wait for this last load to come off?"

The young man smiled, touching his black-gloved fingers to his new cap. "No problem, sir. You've been most cooperative. As soon as your men have driven the trucks down to the end of the pier, I think that'll about do it." He looked at his watch, turning to one of the men behind him, "Hey, fellas, we still got time to catch part of the first quarter."

The men smiled, nodded.

Minutes later, the four trucks rolled slowly down the pier, away from the ship, Valbonne and Saraga's men teaming to move the huge machines, slowly, carefully, a few hundred yards through the darkness. The trucks turned the corner and disappeared behind another warehouse. The men would park there and wait for orders.

Two of the uniformed men stood at the foot of the ship's gangplank, talking to Captain Ohara and First Mate Kuriya, their voices low, a flashlight on the clipboard as answers were taken down.

Valbonne relaxed. He turned to Saraga, who stared at

the uniformed men. The limousine was warm, and the two men enjoyed the heat, knowing that outside the expensive car, it was cold and dark for anybody unfortunate enough to be there. "See?" said the Frenchman. "No gunplay, no problem. They'll be gone in minutes."

"Your Indian works hard," said Saraga. "He has been in the warehouse counting the money most diligently."

Valbonne chuckled. "Yes, he does work hard. Interesting man, Mangas. Six years with him and at times I still don't know what he's thinking. Berk. Now there's a different story. He's easy to figure out. Right now, he's on board your ship, wondering if he's going to live through this. Nothing else is on his mind, and I know that for a fact. I could tell him the answer. The answer is that he isn't."

Saraga turned to look at Valbonne. "Your Indian, what would he do if I tried to cheat you out of the money?"

Valbonne smiled, looking straight ahead at Saraga's chauffeur, sitting motionless in the front seat. "You know the answer."

Saraga nodded once. He knew the answer.

Valbonne leaned forward, looking out of the window to his right. The polite young officer was again walking toward the car, a silly grin on his face. Valbonne kept his smile, though it was dark and the smile probably couldn't be seen. Young fool. More questions, or more hockey scores. Valbonne didn't know which.

He smiled, rolling down the window.

Robert Sand leaned back in the shadows of another warehouse door, his all-black garb making him invisible in the darkness. This abandoned pier on Toronto's waterfront was used rarely, an excellent site to load a small but powerful atomic bomb on trucks and drive it across the border and down into New York City.

It was also the best place to stop the bomb from going any farther.

That's why tonight was his, his plan, his one chance.

As he watched the four trucks come slowly around the corner toward him, his mind moved backward. He had wanted to avoid the bomb exploding through careless gunfire or perhaps a crash of some kind. Even without the trigger and timing device hooked up, the bomb was still highly dangerous.

So the black Samurai's shrewd mind had shown the results of his training under Master Konuma. The four uniformed men off the Canadian police boat were American Secret Service men led by blond, polite and tough Frank Pines. Pines had icewater in his veins. He would do what the Baron had ordered, and the Baron had ordered him to do what Robert Sand wanted done. Pines was one of those men who functioned best when told what to do.

The first part of the plan was completed. The four trucks were away from the warehouse, temporarily out of sight of Valbonne and Saraga. A few hundred yards away from the two, but out of sight. Temporarily. Only temporarily. With only a handful of men and himself, the black Samurai had to rely on cunning, surprise, speed.

He would also use his Samurai training. That's why he had faced death just days ago, beating it back. For now.

The trucks rolled to a stop, heavy wheels pressing hard against the worn wooden pier. He watched and waited.

Then—

Truck doors opened, and men jumped down, stretching, talking quietly among themselves, smoking, laughing. He couldn't see them all, just the men nearest the first two trucks. Four.

Japanese and European.

That meant two to four more. At least six, possibly eight. Three of the Baron's men hid in the darkness with Sand. They hid behind half-closed doors, behind packing cases, each man with a length of iron pipe and a handgun. Sand's Colt .45 hung butt down in a black shoulder holster, and his short sword was shoved diagonally through his waistband in the small of his back.

His fingers brushed his right side, feeling the stiffness of the bandages under the black turtleneck wool sweater. His left forearm was bandaged from wrist to elbow.

His men were watching carefully. The signal would be a small pebble tossed by Sand over the heads of the drivers and onto the wooden pier. The attack was to be silent. No gunplay unless a life depended on it. Use the pipes, take the drivers out quick and hard. Don't stop until they were all on the ground.

Sand took the pebble from his pocket, breathed deeply,

then exhaled. The pebble arched high in the air, hitting the wood and rolling.

Almost before it had stopped rolling, he had reached the four men standing and leaning on the first truck. He attacked them with speed and power, ruthlessly running through them like terrible vengeance rushing out of the darkness.

He shoved his stiff fingers into one man's groin, grabbing his testicles, twisting hard, then pulling back and up. The knife edge of his right hand sliced into the throat of a squat Japanese, once, twice, then Sand spun around, smashing his elbow up and under the jaw of a fat German, knocking the man backward into the side of the truck.

He heard other sounds of struggle around him, but his mind quickly blocked them out. One more man. Sand grabbed the man's right arm, spinning him around, twisting the right hand up high until the fist was between the man's shoulder blades. The fingers of Sand's left hand dug into the man's throat, preventing an outcry, and when he shoved the man swiftly and brutally into the door of the dusty gray truck, Sand quickly moved his own left hand out of the way.

The man fell forward to his knees, his face a bloody horror.

The black Samurai's head turned toward the other truck drivers and the Secret Service men. Quickly, he ran forward toward them.

Frank Pines walked toward the limousine, turning behind him as he walked to watch two of his men still talking to Ohara and Kuriya. Just as Sand had planned. Pines had to hand it to that cool black dude. Goddam foxy mind. Reaching the limousine, he said, "We're 'bout ready to pull out, sir. Want to thank you for your help. Say, this is some car. What kind of steering you got?"

Valbonne smiled, shrugging, always polite. "I don't understand these things. I sit, I ride, that is enough for me."

Pines stroked the car, his eyes looking at it with pleasure. In seconds he was around on the driver's side. "Say, wonder if you could let me look at the steering wheel before I go." He smiled an open, friendly smile.

The Japanese chauffeur, speaking no English, turned his thick neck to look at Saraga. Pines opened the door, his eyes on the steering wheel. The chauffeur's back was to him, and Pines heard the whirring of the glass partition as it slid down and Saraga, still hidden in darkness, spoke a few words in Japanese. As the glass partition slid back up, the chauffeur turned, smiling at Pines, his thick hands touching the shiny brown plastic wheel, his big head bobbing up and down in open friendship.

Pines' eyes grew hard and he quickly looked out of the corner of his left eye into the darkness. His nod was almost imperceptible, but it was as though he had seen something in the blackness that he had been looking for.

His right hand came up swiftly, unseen in the darkness, jabbing the hypodermic needle into the chauffeur's left side, sending the colorless liquid racing through the man's blood toward his heart and brain.

Still smiling, Frank Pines stepped back, slammed the door, lifted a hand in friendly thanks, saying, "Appreciate that. Thanks."

Turning, he raced toward the warehouse just as the harsh headlights came out of the darkness and the roar of a huge truck almost deafened him. The truck picked up speed, bobbing as it hit bumps and holes on the old abandoned pier. The lights grew brighter, the sound of the truck grew louder, and no one seemed to notice. Except Frank Pines, who was getting out of the way as fast as his former all-American basketball legs could take him.

Valbonne and Saraga talked quietly among themselves, the chauffeur sitting silently in front of them. When the light came into the limousine, Valbonne squinted, his hands going to his eyes to shut out the glare. Saraga frowned, then leaned forward, tapping the glass partition.

CHAPTER 18

Death Song

Robert Sand jammed the truck's accelerator to the floor, his strong hands gripping the wheel, fighting it, fighting the pain in his side as the truck jerked, bounced, and made him grit his teeth against the agony he had felt for too many hours.

His eyes were on the limousine, his face grim and determined. He braced himself and smashed into the front of the limousine, speeding as fast as the truck could go, pushing the long black expensive car back along the pier and over the side. The crunch of metal on metal echoed in the night and the car floated only for seconds before it went loudly bubbling down and into the black water.

The two Secret Service men with Ohara and Kuriya had guns pressed against each man's head. "Anybody comes down that gangplank, and you're dead. Both of you. We see one man, we kill you both. That's our orders, and we get paid for carrying out orders. Tell your men your lives are in their rice bowl, Jack." That was Richard DeTorres, Cuban and a man who owed the Baron more than a day's pay. It was the Baron who had smuggled his wife and child out of Cuba and gotten DeTorres into the Secret Service. DeTorres owed the Baron, and he was looking for a chance to pay back.

The crew on board ship came to the rail and stood in the darkness like so many silhouettes, listening to their captain speak to them in Japanese. A flashlight held by DeTorres' partner panned along their faces. No one moved. Everyone listened. "You're a smooth talker, captain," said DeTorres. "Too bad."

Sand leaped from the truck and ran to the edge of the pier, light from the truck's broken headlights coating the water in pale yellow where the limousine had gone under.

When the bodies were discovered, an autopsy would show the chauffeur had had a heart attack. There would be no marks on either Saraga or Valbonne. As for the crushed fender and dented front of the car, let whoever was interested in it figure it out.

Sand's head snapped toward the sound of gunfire.

In the half-light coming from the warehouse, he saw Frank Pines lying prone on the ground, stomach on the wooden pier, legs apart, two hands gripping a .45. Spread out near him were two other men, each in the same position.

Pines' head turned in time to see the black Samurai crouch down near him. "Jesus, man," said Pines. "Don't you ever make noise when you move?"

Sand's eyes were on the warehouse.

He heard Pines say, "We dropped two of them for sure, and we may have hit somebody else. Like you planned, we caught them running through the front door to check out the noise. I'm not taking any chances with your Apache friend in there, not after the way he sicked his little house pet on you back in Geneva. Anyway, your plan's working. A-OK, so far. I'd feel a hell of a lot happier though, if I knew that Indian was dancing around heaven."

Sand said nothing. Then—"I'm going in."

"You what?"

"Tell everybody to fire into the warehouse. Knock out as many lights as possible. When I say *now*, stop, and I mean stop."

Pines nodded. Orders. What the hell.

He leaned back on his left side, waved an arm to the two men lying on the ground near him, then signaled them to shoot. They did, the noise of their heavy handguns roaring again and again, the orange flames flashing for an instant in the blackness, then disappearing.

Sand yelled down at Pines. "Now!"

Pines stopped firing, then cupped his hands to his mouth, turning to his men. "That's it! That's it!"

When he turned, the black Samurai had disappeared.

Salt was on his knees, leaning against the dirty warehouse wall. His left hand pressed hard against his side, trying to push the blood back into his body. His hand felt wet, warm, and the pain had slid away, leaving just numbness. Shit, it wasn't all that bad. Hell, getting shot ain't shit.

He gritted his teeth, the sweat beading along his darkbrown face. He still didn't know what was going on out there. Lot of noise though, man, a hell of a lot of noise. Car crashes, gunfire, guys getting wasted beside him, and some dudes outside trying to blow everybody away. Damn! He had walked right into a bullet.

He closed his eyes, squeezing them tightly, then opening them wide, still seeing darkness. The hurt was coming back now, and he fought against it as hard as he could. Apache. A good sound, that word. Apache warrior. He jerked, then stiffened with the pain.

Noises. Did he hear something?

"Salt."

Somebody was calling his name. Or was he hearing things?

"Salt." There it was again. He had heard the old men of his tribe talk about dying, about how sometimes you saw things like Life Giver, the Apache God. Or White Painted Woman. She was also God. But that happened when—

He moved away from his spot in the darkness, always the crafty warrior.

"Salt."

He wasn't hearing things. And his eyes grew wide with wonder and a touch of fear. He knew. He knew without having to see. He could hear his own heart beat faster. His lips were dry. He licked them. "Samurai. It's you. I know it's you." His own voice sounded far away, and he moved again, each inch crawled in the darkness paining him.

"Yes. I want to ask you something. I know you have lived as an Apache warrior. I understand that. I respect that. Do you want to surrender? Do you want to live?"

Salt reached a packing case. He pulled himself behind it, leaning against the wood. He listened to Sand's soft voice coming out of the darkness. Man, some dude. Rattlesnake bite and still breathing. Too much.

"Valbonne is dead. So is Saraga. There is no one else

alive or conscious in this warehouse but you and me. Men are out front with guns. They don't want to take you alive, but I can see that you live if you want to."

Salt took off his shirt, each movement paining him, and balled it up, pressing it hard against his side. Valbonne dead. There was a small sadness in him at that, but he pushed it away.

He breathed deeply, his bare chest and face wet with perspiration. He looked up at the ceiling and saw only two dim, dirty yellow bulbs still giving off light. His left hand held his now-bloody shirt, his right gripped his ax. To live from now on was *not* to live as a warrior. To die now was to remain an Apache warrior. Forever. Better death than life in a cage. In death, he could join his brother warriors.

And the only man who understood that was a man he had called enemy, but a man more his brother than anyone else he had met since his own Apache people. The one man who understood, and now he and that man were locked in a death struggle. It was too late for it to be different.

The black Samurai crouched in darkness, his eyes on the packing case. He stayed away from the meager, dim yellow light.

Suddenly, he tensed as he heard the sound. A high-pitched chant coming from behind the case. "Hi-yi-yi-yi-yi, Hi-yi-yi-yi-yi." An eerie song, a haunting, frightening, incredibly sad sound. The Apache's death chant. That was his answer to Robert Sand.

Salt wanted to die as an Apache warrior. He would die fighting.

The packing case clattered in the night, pushed aside and to the floor by the waning strength of the huge, bleeding Apache. In the darkness, he stood tall, the ax gripped tightly in his hand, his eyes burning with the spirit of a great race of warriors.

Bleeding and in pain, stumbling in the darkness, he sang his death song and charged, not knowing where Sand was. His strained voice rose higher with the Apache death chant.

The black Samurai cleared his short sword from the scabbard and stood up to meet the Apache warrior. Sand's voice was sad. "Here, my brother," he said softly.

Sand stood in the huge open door of the warehouse, the body of Mangas Salt held effortlessly in his arms. Frank Pines and other Secret Service men walked slowly toward them.

"There's $50 million back there," said Sand. "I want it burned. All of it. Burned. Because of that money, people were going to die. I don't want anyone ever using it or seeing it." His voice was flat, and there was no room for argument. He looked at Frank Pines, who nodded his head once.

The black Samurai walked past them, stepping from the light and deeper and deeper into the darkness. He walked slowly, the huge Indian's lifeless arms dangling freely. In the darkness, no one saw Sand's tears.

The Baron chuckled. "I've heard of people going through money like water, but damn, son, like fire? Frank told me why, and well, maybe you got a point."

"Thanks." Sand finished packing and closed the small brown suitcase. Turning to the Baron, he said, "How long have I got?"

"Three days—72 hours. Then you're due in Spain. So far, three of my men have been killed on this one. I don't wanna hear a goddam thing about number four."

"I'll try."

"Son, lemme ask you. Why are you goin' back to Geneva for just a few hours of fun and frolic? I mean, Zoraida's a tasty morsel, but you could stay here in New York and enjoy yourself just as well."

Sand's smile was grim. "I don't know if I've got three days, three years or even three hours of life left to me. But whatever it is, I want to hold on to it for as long or as short a time as I can. I came close to cashing in this time. It's not her, so much. She just happens to be around, that's all."

"Well, she's a lucky little lady to have you and me. You for what you're about to do to her when you get your hands on her, and me for gettin' her a $2,000-a-month public-relations job in Paris. Ain't I a sweetheart, though?" He chuckled softly.

Sand walked over to the Baron. He looked at him for several seconds, seeing the keen blue eyes, the tanned, lined face of the Texan who had the courage to care about so many things. "Thanks," he said and turned away.

Sand could have said more, but didn't. It would have been difficult. The Baron had had Mangas Salt's body shipped back to Arizona, arranging for the burial, doing it secretly, quietly, seeing that the Apache was buried high in the mountains of Arizona.

Sand walked through the door, closing it behind him. Someone besides himself cared about an Apache warrior.

More SIGNET Books You'll Want to Read

☐ **SEE THE WOMAN by Dallas Barnes.** More devastating than **The New Centurions!** A brutally honest, torridly paced novel about the Los Angeles police—by a cop on the inside of the action. (#Y5529—$1.25)

☐ **THE PATROLMAN: A COP'S STORY by Edward F. Droge, Jr.** A shattering book that takes you into the squad cars, the precinct houses, the alleyways—and into a policeman's very guts. (#Y5468—$1.25)

☐ **THE PRIVATE SECTOR by Joseph Hone.** A brilliant and calculated spy story of callous political and human intrigue—double and triple agents on the London-Moscow circuit, denizens of the dark alleyways of Cairo during the weeks leading up to the Six-Day War. "Absolutely chilling, enthralling."—**Boston Globe** (#Y5463—$1.25)

☐ **COPS AND ROBBERS by Donald E. Westlake.** Catch the crime of the year as two cool cops pull off the hottest heist since **The Hot Rock!** A smash United Artists film starring Cliff Gorman and Joseph Bologna.
(#Y5892—$1.25)

☐ **SICILIAN DEFENSE by John Nicholas Iannuzzi.** On one side was the most powerful Sicilian Family in New York, with an interest in every form of illegal money-making in the metropolis. On the other side was a ruthless and determined black organization intent on carving out its own underworld empire. In the middle waited the city. **Sicilian Defense**—the book that begins where **The Godfather** left off! (#Y5488—$1.25)